JOHN C. TARPEY

IN SUSPENSION

SHORT STORIES + TYPE TANGENTS

authorHOUSE®

AuthorHouse™ UK
1663 Liberty Drive
Bloomington, IN 47403 USA
www.authorhouse.co.uk
Phone: 0800.197.4150

Published by AuthorHouse 02/27/2019

ISBN: 978-1-7283-8501-3 (sc)
ISBN: 978-1-7283-8505-1 (e)

Library of Congress Control Number: 2018913701

Print information available on the last page.

TO HELEN AND SEAMUS

Born in 1969, John Tarpey was raised in Kiltimagh, Co. Mayo. His research preferences include typographic experimentation and the visual interpretation of written content. Currently working as a full time lecturer of Graphic Design at the Waterford Institute of Technology.

Contents

CHAPTER

1

WEATHER

| |!|:|;|.|,|?|-|""|()|

• • •

On a good day, the bank of dull cloud settled into layers of dark blue smoke. None of these layers motioned to move down the sentry hill and storm the town. Stone-faced, looming like the injured party in a dispute preparing to say their final words, winter was drawn out and predictable. Traffic had chased itself down to a few nervous coughs from a delivery van desperate to keep its cab warm. Side roads braced themselves for the afternoon school run panic. School-mom motorists cruised Main Street, reminding pedestrians with little mouths to feed to stock up on weekly provisions. Midweek afternoons allowed older people or those living alone to move around with ease, avoiding the weekend shopping assault.

Weather couldn't compromise or be taught a new point of view. It defied every one of our pleas for a rosy glimpse of the sun. Nope, it would never let us play too long with it, regardless of our promise to give the bright ball back. West-of-Ireland weather wouldn't give in. Not one inch. It just gave us a cheeky backward stare, as if to imply that we owed it something first. Every so often it tossed us a day or two reprieve to lift the essence of our idle banter. Before we even attempted our ritual parting of bedroom curtains, the western side of the country cautiously prepared itself. The ecstasy of being proved wrong was rare. We were all slaves to its seasonal whims. Until we acknowledged it, we could never work around it. Miserable, mean weather.

Weather in the West always changed quickly. It could make you take your eye off the ball. Chasing words vibrantly away from holy-shit wows, corralling them like wet cattle onto the doorsteps of hah and huh? Bad days created nothing more than damp coat shoulders and screwed-up eyes. Miserable, mean weather. So bad that it couldn't be employed as a deflection from awkward moments. Drifting in and out of thought from lack of chat, the Aloof's mind imagined yellow Post-its to his internal script, one planned in the hope that an opportune moment would finally reveal its secret. Maybe a lack of planning was what made this little country so innovative? Planning was what the locals used bad weather for.

Imaginary yellow Post-its of meaning, the clever type, would soon flutter in and around the dulled consciousness of Maguire's bar. Any breath of fresh air of positivity, any breeze-flinching of a good idea, could be blown away by peer rejection or ill-informed bravado. Most Post-its were unable to adhere to the carriage windowpane of his departing train of thought. His latest idea might just stick. One simple idea, close to realisation, fought the cries of the wind and addictive smartphone checks of others. The elderly used the time to reflect on ideas that needed adjusting. They knew the irony of technological distraction. The youth these days had no patience and so no concept for playing the long game.

Lone daytime drinkers sat and contemplated their tragic timelines, right up until their present demise. They searched for some small historic trace of enlightenment. Some clue to a potential solution that would release them from whatever trouble they'd gotten into. Always telling themselves the answer was right there in front of them, just waiting for them to make the connection. It might be just a simple observation. Maybe something as simple as recognising the strange similarities between Stevie Wonder's 'Very Superstitious' and Peter Gabriel's 'Sledge Hammer'. The wail of the wind could cripple pleasurable thoughts easily and then trail away as if nothing had happened. Alcohol manipulated memories badly before storing them in parts of the mind where recall was unreliable.

Miserable, mocking weather. When it eventually decided to interrupt your daily routine, or cancelled an important chore, it allowed you to scream outrageous obscenities at it. If you dared to describe it truthfully or tried to dig deep for appropriate vulgarities, it tossed you into a heap of confusion. When you think you're in control of your life, you might be able to assess the weather as it presents itself, but only in the moment. It won't let you put your finger on it, easily side-stepping your demands from every angle, eventually getting under your skin to chill the bone right through. Respect for Irish weather is wise. It will play you like a tumbleweed on a hot deserted highway and dismiss you faster than a scarecrow's smile.

Wednesday was a day for weirdness. Marauding wrecks from the weekend braved the downpour to make their way into Maguire's for afternoon pints. The hope of getting a sub, a monetary loan, from an acquaintance of recent making was how the man they called 'the Sub' operated. Dennis, the owner of Maguire's, would double-check the stacks of coins presented by the Sub. He checked every time. The man's coins tried to convince every barman in town that they rarely graced hardwood counters for booze. Collecting the small currency, Dennis made it obvious to all punters within earshot that every single cent belonging to their local pest had been examined closely and counted correctly.

The go-to subject matter for sustainable small talk, weather, was of interest when all other subject matter failed or wore thin from repetition. It could rekindle forgotten glories of present day heroes and finite stories of loss. Teasing collective memories which may have been unquestioned for too long. The Players, who held their own territory in the bar, had no interest in such observations. They had little to no tolerance for idle chit-chat. The Players must have ongoing interesting lives and tales to tell. The Aloof was a total stranger. He could quickly ascertain which local was popular or unpopular, friend or foe to the Players, by their weather chatter. Some barely audible murmur or disposable insult would do it. The Players were far too important, all conversation had to revolve around them.

Loans of a few euros were not to be found in Maguire's bar. No disposable cash these days. Not from the Players: you'd have to be a long-time member. They never gave loans, and they would never let you forget asking them. The Sub knew the first of three pints might have to be nursed to the point of sourness. Couldn't appear to be wanting. The noise of pebble-dash rain on the large front window forced the Sub to stay. Everyone in the bar was a hostage today. A potential sub may lie in the pocket of the Aloof, but his distracted stare might only respond to the second attempt to get his attention. The art of securing a sub depended on the patience of the predator once the weakest of the herd had been selected.

The Sub looked out of the large front window and smiled. The weather was in league with him today. He knew these conditions could play a crucial part in the timing of his plea for a few quid. You'd only squeeze two pints from a tenner, which had become the new fiver. If today's weather kept its demonic wind integrity, then his approach might be concealed from the Players. The Aloof was under observation, his drinking speed being assessed. It would determine whether he was likely to continue drinking or leave the bar soon. The young man's habits and body language did not specifically make him a target. Being a stranger here today, did.

The seventy-five-year-old front door strained at its brass hinges, allowing an occasional gust to shoot through the bar like some cold Doberman off its leash. The chill went straight for the knees and bone-rattled all those who were recovering from an illness. The perfect distraction for the Sub to make a move towards the Aloof. Leaning across the bar counter, Dennis advised the Players to bring their alert status up to periscope levels. Which torpedo would be employed today? It needed to be some plausible tale of woe. The Players reckoned he'd pick one of his tried-and-tested Sub stories. Something simple rather than stretching the imagination. The stranger was going to have to leave the bar sometime soon.

The Sub's approach today started with a casual walk past the Aloof, allegedly to gauge the ferocity of the wind. The young man, still trapped in his concentrated personal exploration, recoiled dramatically on his bar stool. The wind assisted opening the front door and caught all customers off guard but one. 'My dog wouldn't dare go out in that,' said the Sub, who'd never owned a dog. His voice, calm and smoky in its delivery, was aimed in the direction of the Aloof. The Players pretended not to notice. It was a predictable opening line. A slow dejected walk followed, until he stopped shoulder side with the Aloof, who was still lost in some lazy thought. A perfect chance set him up to pounce. 'You wouldn't be heading anywhere near Flanagan's Hill by any chance? I'm a bit fecked, and it would be safer to get a lift.'

It took a moment for the Aloof to rejoin his surroundings. The chorus of the wind and petrified door slams had staying power. 'Sorry? I'm from the town,' he replied, avoiding any eye contact. Though it was spoken with a convincing youthful naivety, the Aloof made sure he had sucker written all over his face. The Players watched the pair, knowing that the Sub was a native from the town too. A fiver or a €10 note was about to vanish from the wallet of the Aloof. A likely guess would be taxi fare. A plausible weather-related story, no doubt. No need to dig too deep into his backlog of lies. A perfectly horrible day outside was a good enough excuse. The Players groaned on hearing the old and familiar taxi line.

A battered black leather wallet with notes of a specific blue slipped from the pocket of the Aloof. A swift back slap of appreciation from the Sub and a hasty turn on his heels. Twenty euros secured with extreme ease, he thought with glee. Internalising a victory howl, the Sub braced himself for his exit into the drilling wind and rain. Drawing his attention with their lack of chatter, the Players power-stared down the bar at the Aloof with dismissive headshakes. He sensed their safety-in-numbers ridicule was ready to kick off, but he didn't appear too concerned. It began with a tut-tutting by Dennis, who wondered if the Sub got much … €20? His mock-pause stare was meant to be unnerving and unwelcome. According to the Players, this pause was depriving them of their beer. The Aloof was unimpressed and held his distant composure.

'Wha'd'ya reckon, men? If I was a betting man, I'd say it looks like bucko here has been conned by our old friend, the Sub.' He happily tapped the empty bar counter beside the Aloof. 'You're another victim. Now I hope you realise that you won't be seeing any of that money again. It's gone bye-bye, baby!'

For once the sound of the Players' laughter could compete with the latest gust of the wind outside. To their surprise, the Aloof majestically stood up, pushed his bar stool back into its proper position, and approached the group of five Players, who were hoping for another chance to laugh at his expense.

Any person concealing an ace up his sleeve has a controlling presence in the face of public ridicule. Though there could be unforeseen consequences, the Players were growing in confidence and eager to call his bluff.

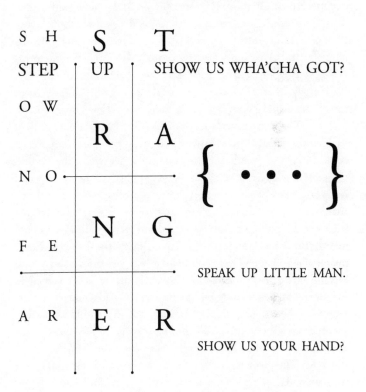

There is security in having a plan, especially if it's one that had been considered and tweaked for months. He had no choice but to embrace the smirking intimidation from the other end of the bar.

'The Sub, where will he go to next?' the young man asked. 'I mean which bar will he go to next? It's important ... c'mon tell me.'

The Players looked at each other as if to say, The boy's got a pair. Dennis proposed that Morty's would be the most likely choice.

'Ring Morty's, and tell them to be on the lookout for a fake twenty euro note in the next few minutes,' said the Aloof confidently.

Stunned by their initial misreading of the youth, the Players became intrigued by his unexpected cunning. Dennis phoned Morty's with a Garda Síochána matter-of-fact tone to his voice, ending the call with an accurate description of the Sub. He happily returned to the pod, upbeat and thrilled to be part of something. Mind games ... they're so much better than board games.

The Players, with fresh drinks in front of them and led by Dennis, saluted this creative young stranger. Dennis retrieved the remnants of the Aloof's pint from the other end of the bar and placed it beside the Players. Join them, young man, he implied and indicated that there was a free pint in the till when he'd finished that one. Introductions led to explanations. The Aloof's father's shop got dodgy notes every so often, and he was allowed to have one Robin Hood opportunity regarding their disposal. Some people you just knew were con men; others you only heard about. A shop was a perfect place to find out. The Aloof explained to his captive audience in detail how to identify the counterfeit note.

The Aloof gave a fresh dud note to Dennis with strict instructions that if the Sub came back to con another stranger, he should prep the victim first. Then they were to inform the Sub that Hennessey's (who would be warned) had a happy hour that day. The Players realised that the Aloof had thought through this scenario for quite some time. The young man had heard that the Sub recently squeezed money from an elderly neighbour, an old gent, who was too generous, too polite, or too scared to refuse his demands. The youngster had wished for this for some time but figured that progress took too long to materialise in this town. The Sub relied on this slowness of justice.

The Players couldn't resist asking Dennis for a second phone call to Morty's, just to find out whether the Sub had fallen foul of the mighty fake note. Too excited to process recalcitrant buttons, Dennis's digit dangled and became numerically amnesic. The others tried desperately to explain the nature and function of the recall button. Technology was not exactly his strong point. He came from a family that felt they needed nostalgia to keep the till ringing. Displaying leadership but no patience, one Player brazenly walked behind the bar counter and took control. Dennis winked towards the others, indicating his success at conveying incompetence. The Players never wanted to be included in his jokes.

'Hi, Barry, Dennis here again. Yeah, just a quick question. Did you, by any chance, get any fake twenties today? Ah-ha, well I'm looking at one now right here in front of me. I do, I do indeed!'

Dennis couldn't help pretending he was clueless. He got a kick out of it even if nobody appreciated his efforts. He continued. 'Oh right, I can see those very same marks here. We just got the tip-off here a few minutes ago. Who? Well if it had to be anyone, it would have to be him. No, Barry, that makes complete sense to me. It's just in his nature, I guess. Well, as we know, times are tough and he's bound to get creative. He left here a while ago. Is he still with you lot? No, but a quick ring around to the other bars wouldn't do any harm. A true pest. No bother, Barry … G'luck!'

He returned to face the expectant expressions of the Players and enjoyed some theatrical teasing by refusing to reveal the specifics of the phone conversation. But eagerly waiting for one of them to crack had backfired before. None of them budged. 'Well, I do believe that the wheels are definitely in motion,' he said. 'I think we owe this young man our thanks.'

A glass of hope was raised to the Aloof. The Players could tell the Aloof was not relaxing, cautious of their company. He had to focus on the ultimate prize. Catching this rogue meant discrediting his money. All money in his possession must have its value debased, its fiscal credibility removed in the eyes of all whom he dealt with.

The Players lived to be entertained by situations like this. They warmed from tepid to extra cosy. Weather took a back seat to the retelling of some of the Sub's historic feats. There were times when he wasn't so bad, just a chancer. Feigned sincerity and harmless lying that eventually grew to be pathological. He had a gift back then and could cloak his intentions with such innocence. The Players laughed. The dodgy note had become a powerful symbol of their resistance against the Sub. They could wave a crisp €20 note in front of his face whenever they saw him and chase him away like a vampire. There would be great mileage out of this simple sting. The Players had always embraced all excuses for exorcising boredom.

Amidst the intermittent laughter, the Aloof was struck by an uncomfortable query and ventured to interrupt the Players' fun. All apologetic, he asked Dennis if Morty's had accepted the fake note or given it back to the Sub. His concern was that if the Sub had been refused and the note was confiscated, it wouldn't be long before he'd be on the move, looking for more money. Maybe he'd be knocking on his old neighbour's door. The Aloof explained that, according to word in the shop, his neighbour was living in fear because a bunch of psychos had just moved in next door to him. The Sub preyed on the poor man's fears and claimed he'd protect him. That was how he'd been extracting money from him. By their facial expressions and wind-wail pitch, the severity of the Players' disdain for the Sub was clear. They froze in unison. A silent realisation, based on a common knowledge. 'The Suit,' said Dennis. 'I mean, your neighbour is the Suit?'

The Aloof had to wait until the Players gestured to him that he should continue. Recall button pushed, and with an assertive clearance of his throat, Dennis prepared his phone persona once more. 'Barry? It's only me again ... no it's Dennis, you idiot. Just another quick question, sorry to annoy you. Did you cash the twenty or did he keep it? Right. Just one more quick question: has the Suit been in your place lately? Was he there today? He wasn't? No, just checking. He's been getting a bit quiet lately, that's all.'

The phone call continued through a repetitive roll of ah-has and yeahs until an end was brokered by mutual consent. The fake €20 note was still in the Sub's possession. Barry had also mentioned that the Gardaí had been ringing around, quizzing the other bars about the fake twenties. Dennis relayed to the Players that the face on the Sub was priceless when he heard this. It seemed that he left Barry's place in a huff, confused and very definitely angry. 'Lads, if the Sub is that annoyed, he might do something stupid. The fool might try and shake down the Suit,' said Dennis. The Aloof had a similar thought and interjected with gusto.

'Hold it, would one of you drive me up there? The Suit knows me from the shop. I mean, he gets on with me. I've an idea.'

The Players gave their new buddy the floor once more. The Aloof's plan was to give the frightened man a dodgy €50 note. The Suit would have to convince the Sub that he had just won the €50 from a quick-pick lotto ticket in Larry's shop earlier. Because the note was won, the Sub would probably assume that it was legit and would work to get it from him. 'All of you split up now. Get yourselves to bars that the Sub drinks in. Visit his usual haunts and keep an eye on his reaction when he gets refused. One guy needs to park near the Suit's house just in case the Sub gets aggressive. The key to this plan is that the Suit must not get damaged and the Sub gets barred trying to pass the €50 for drink,' said the Aloof intensely.

'How come you (pointing at all The Players) never came up with ideas like this kid?' asked Dennis with exaggerated game show gesticulation and a terrible mid-Atlantic accent. The Players laughed begrudgingly at their in-house jester, but they were at a loss to come up with an honest answer. They had grown up in a different era when you dealt with problems face to face.

The Sub would probably backtrack each pub until he could replace the dud note with clean notes. It might mean scraping together a clean tenner to give him enough time to prey on another victim. The idea of being singled out as the only bearer of fraudulent notes might not bother a rogue like the Sub.

One of the non-drinkers in the Player's corner kindly volunteered to drive the Aloof over to the Suit's house. He encouraged all those remaining to move quickly into position. Climatic conditions outside were dismissed. The Players' concern for the Suit seemed slightly abnormal. Maybe they showed concern today so that they didn't get accused of being unwilling to help when they could have. They had always wanted to be perceived as being part of the right team when it really mattered. This moment might prove to be a glorious opportunity for all of them to show their willingness to participate in an act of community concern.

Dennis watched the Aloof and the volunteer depart before he posed an obvious question to the three Players that stayed behind. What was his name, the young mastermind? They could place the face from years of popping into Larry's shop, but knowing everyone's name was of little importance now. This last hour had been more entertaining than usual, and it hadn't ended yet. More important, it could be proven that the Players had been there at the start, observed the plan and its evolution, and now they might be privy to its conclusion. This simple episode had classic community folklore potential written all over it. A story that could withstand poor storytelling, embellishment, and complete inaccuracy. The remaining three Players eagerly waited to act on demand, knowing their current reputations were still intact.

Weather granted a solid reason for waiting, so there were no signs of vigilante tendencies amongst the Players that remained. No audible rise in arrogance. Now the only thing that would listen to the Sub was the weather. Miserable, mean weather. It wouldn't accept his feeble excuses nor his pleas of innocence, atonement, or justice. It couldn't care who got what was coming to them or how appropriate their comeuppance happened to be. Weather did not and never would take anything personally. Like those business-as-usual signs still swinging on storm-damaged shops, it just went on. There would always be another Sub waiting to pounce, just like there would always be miserable, mean weather.

2

TIMING

| | |:|;|.|,|?|-|"""|()|

!

Soaked in the reverence of an old Sunday suit, an elderly man sat alone in the least festive corner of the bar. Nobody knew if it was his last-ditch effort to maintain visibility amongst the haze of his elderly peers. He and others like him had been asked to move out of the way. Socialising was just another funeral he felt obliged to attend. Morty's was his only local bar simply because it was closest. Meet-and-greet rituals helped revise and update the family trees of his friends, both living and departed. He had been a settled widower for several years. No family, not since the passing of his wife, and now the basic need for human contact did not rate as high. This was especially true after another anonymous, dysfunctional couple moved into the house next door. The Suit's new neighbours had relocated their fighting from somewhere else, producing two-fingered salutes to his passing hellos before slamming their front door. Gut instinct told him that they wouldn't accept any attempt at a sincere welcome and half salutes of basic politeness were a waste of what energy he had left. Their community spirit might have got misplaced during the move? The constant shouting may indicate that both were raised by big families in small houses on a street of similar-sized families. That upbringing taught you to keep two sets of eyes in your head but didn't do much for the sense of trust in the neighbourhood. The old man was forced to keep his mind on his own business lately.

These days the Suit organised his movements to avoid contact with the couple next door. According to his logic, his new neighbours could enter and exit their house without having to stop, look at, or listen to him. Their gate settled to a stop eventually after being slammed. That was their cue to him that he could leave. The pair could watch him walk away without fear of his looking back. Their rented house was not one you chose. An old building, it cowered behind a distressed hedge, neglected and bent out of shape. It had become a cheap stage for their soap opera. The Suit prayed that this pair would move out soon because he couldn't wait for common sense to intervene.

Over time the Suit developed a defeated posture and bowed head when walking the short garden path to his front door. It didn't help his cause much. As soon as the couple heard the Suit fumbling for his front door keys, they deliberately cranked up the stereo to make the old man flinch. They made sure he heard them laugh. It was becoming a base level form of intimidation, and the couple was clearly getting the hang of it. Their game had crossed the city limits of nastiness now and had moved on to playing psychological chicken with their neighbour's nerves. Thugs loved to push. His generation grew up surviving on very little and never asking others for help, never mind accepting it.

'That pair of nutters are going to give that man a heart attack one of these days.' The regulars in the local bar were aware of the old man's trouble, but only Barry, the owner, knew the details. Both chose to deal with it through humorous deflection and bar banter. Barry feared the old man's suit would outlast the harmless creature housed within it. The Suit always changed out of his three-piece upon his return home. He needed it to last for a few more months. It was taking care of him. The ritual of putting it on had a reassuring effect each morning. A time would come when appearances could not be maintained any longer. This was not a newly beaten member of society but a person who was in the process of being forced to step aside from it completely.

Recently, the Suit tried not to stay out too late. Nevertheless, the small circle of familiar faces in Morty's could tell that he was reluctant to leave their company. His anxiety was palpable when he had to refuse an offer of a parting drink. Too proud to accept a lift home, he reminded them it was only a five-minute walk. A heartfelt salute at the doorway was always returned with genuine appreciation from the departing soul. The bar grew noticeably cold with the lack of banter. Isolated coughs of concern expressed hope for some voice of reason to put words to their collective fears. Nobody would speak until they were sure the old man was gone. Barry signalled with a nod that the Suit had left the building and was heading home.

The Suit acknowledged his walking pace home had slowed lately, a sign that his mind was in a bad place. He was conscious of how good Morty's was to him because of the badness next door. Strange. No curtain twitch, no silhouette stance, no evidence of activity next door. Everything appeared quiet. Best not tempt fate, not since he'd fooled himself before. It was only half ten and there was plenty of scope for grief yet. Safely inside, he changed into his jogging suit, slow-stepping downstairs to the safety of the kitchen TV. Still his favourite room in the house, as it was further away from them. He didn't want to listen to which mode of violence she'd shriek to avoid or what excuse her boyfriend would later give to Gardaí.

Surely this couldn't be what it meant to survive for this long? A lifetime leading up to an existence like this? Be it work or caring for his wife, was it all worth it to be imprisoned by this situation?

He couldn't move away now. The Gardaí said there was little that they could do until next door did something first. Nobody wanted to get involved these days. Not worth the hassle for fear of retaliation. Most of his friends were dead, in homes for the elderly, or dying a slow death. His depressing train of thought was jackknifed by a horrific scream which penetrated the walls. A symphony of paranoid accusations rained down on the female next door. The Suit wished that Barry could witness the ferocity. It would save him time explaining at his bar counter therapy.

'Lads, our friend the Suit is fading away. His nerves are beginning to fray, all because of a couple of addicts. A pair of wasters who would never do a day's work in their lives. These two have no respect for their next-door neighbour, a gentleman who worked his arse off to pay for all he owns. We all know how he had to take care of his wife for years until her long battle ended. They're grinding him down, lads, and I'm afraid he might fall apart at the seams.'

The Leader had spoken. Nobody responded. They shifted in their seats, knowing that they were being asked to participate in a new crusade. Morty's was the old man's pub of choice also. The Leader sat, drawing his stool nearer to the whispering frowns.

The immediacy with which they had formed a huddle said quite a lot about the depth of their common concern. Solutions that they had heard about, that had worked in the past, were placed on the table. When a plan was hatched, its intention must be established and clarified with the belief that their actions were fully justified. By any means necessary? Was their intention being blinded by hatred for antisocial behaviour or just plain sympathy for the victim? Their solutions were probably based on a mixture of both. The group had divided itself in two. Each group would return the next day and then objectively present their research.

On Thursday evening, both groups returned to the bar as planned. The Leader cleared his throat and respectfully read out the most popular suggestions. The Extroverts were anticipating a win while the Introverts were nervous of the responsibility of losing.

The Extroverts: 87 per cent for and 13 per cent against. 'Let's go and beat several shades of crap out of them or maybe send them a sheep's head with an or-else message tied to it.' The Leader paused to digest that thought. 'Nothing too satanic! Plain, simple and straight to the point. It has potential. Nice touch. That your idea, Pete?' Pete pointed at a petite woman nursing her wine. 'Linda! I'm truly shocked at you. Seriously, people, I'm not sure I want to go to the toilet on my own anymore.'

Linda laughed aggressively and whispered some horrific addition which made her boyfriend pale and cover his mouth. The Introverts: 100 per cent for and an impressive 0 per cent against. The Introverts favoured logic over emotive instincts to prevent embarrassing situations. 'Make contact with the landlord to inform the occupants that the house is being sold. Give them a month's notice to leave the house, and the posse will get a good neighbour to move in to replace them in return for playing ball.'

Simple logic doesn't always satisfy a posse that is looking for drama, but the Introverts pushed to at least try legal routes first. Nobody wanted to end up in the same situation as the Suit, and all of them knew someone elderly who was just as vulnerable.

The Leader spoke calmly to all and without any noticeable preference for either side. Something had to be done; nobody shied away from that fact. The consensus was that they would try the Introverted route first. If that got nowhere then it was on to the sheep's head. Specific roles would have to be assigned to individuals with certain skills. Namely, there were people who could order the head of a sheep (at short notice) without even the remotest intrigue concerning its use. Nobody outside the circle would know the actions of those acting within it. The Introverts feared that the Extroverts would get the circus they so desperately hoped for after all.

It took until Sunday afternoon to get in contact with the thug's landlord, a local man who was surprisingly open to the loss of rent, considering these hard times. He hadn't had a good tenant in years. His reliance on social housing randomness meant he'd get a few bad apples every so often. The current pair of misfits had become an embarrassment, and getting them out was definitely in his favour. The only worry for the landlord was that the troublesome tenants would damage his house as they departed. Nothing had seemed to bother the dangerous duo before this. Well, not that the landlord could see. He could not figure out why the girlfriend was with the thug in the first place.

The fact that this deeply disruptive couple were originally from another urban district persuaded the leader to push for action sooner. Unfortunately, news came back that the thug didn't really feel like moving. He claimed that his girlfriend needed concrete proof that the house was indeed for sale or she'd bring legal action against the landlord. All thugs claim to know their rights, playing the victim card because authorities lack the power to stop them.

'Well, looks like it's going to be the sheep's head, lads,' said the Leader. 'Time to show off your ingenuity and flair for the dramatic. I know you can do it: I've seen you all at weddings.' The Extroverts simply craved attention and the energy drawn from antisocial risk-taking. The Introverts worried that this exercise was no longer concerned with justice for the old man.

Hush Now,

GRAB ALL YOUR DRINKS

WE ONLY HAVE ONE CHANCE AT THIS.

AND LET'S GATHER ROUND

FOCUS

AND BEFORE WE FORGET
THE SUIT IS DEPENDING
ON EACH AND
EVERY ONE OF US.

!

IT'S SERIOUS   •   NO JOKING!

{   }

Linda don't laugh.

'It goes a little something like this', said The Leader. 'Soon as The Suit arrives in I'll ring to give the all clear and do it. Percy's idea of pouring petrol on the sheep's head before the confrontation isn't that bad at all. Whoever leaves the sheep's head at the door must go to the back of the posse before someone else sets it alight, in case of vapours. And don't light it until we make our point clear. Balaclavas and pickaxe handles for good measure. So... one rock through a side window followed by sheep's head ready to set on fire at the door and if the thug doesn't listen or get the hint then, I'll take responsibility for the beating. You all know I'm not a violent man.'

Sunday evening arrived and there was no sign of The Suit. The plan was itching to be put into action. The focal point, the man himself, the key to igniting change in this town was nowhere to be found. It must have been three days ago he was seen last. The Leader wondered if he's away or in hospital? Maybe someone could drive by and check; see if there's a fire on. Linda thought she spotted him at the bus stop but she couldn't be sure. Feedback from the drive-by suggested that there was nobody was at home. This could be an opportune moment to strike. Everybody agreed that it was now or never. Their nerve was collectively solid, there was no going back.

The mob went willingly into attack mode, putting their plan into brutal affect. Some Extroverts secretly felt this moment had been predestined somehow and now they had been given a right to deal with unfinished business from times gone by. Genuine screams of panic soared high at the sight of flaming mutton. The horrific roars of pain extracted from a thug on borrowed time. The window curtain gasps from shocked residents hiding in earshot. All of the elderly hoping that this comeuppance might send a message to all those harbouring similar thoughts of anti-social behaviour. These silent senior citizens never asked their community for much. While they may have eight-second attention spans, they could remember back when Belfast streets had been cleared by systematic torching. This scene reminded them that there were times when it was best not to question whether the aim justified the means.

The vigilantes' departure bore the appearance of military discipline. As many illegal crusades tend to end, the word 'rat' was painted vividly on the door as a visual warning to others. The word might just give the whole episode the appearance of drug feuding. More important, the violence of the event was recorded on a mobile phone to make the victim view it under painful duress. The volume increased as his piercing screams and genuine fear for his girlfriend heightened. The spectacle looked curious to the neighbourhood kids who had gathered outside the house until one balaclava told them that each of them was known. Everybody took heed.

The posse confidently returned to Morty's. The Extroverts were still high, charged, and giddy. Half-sentence excitement and an inability to describe what they were feeling made them chase words in circles. The Introverts, however, were thankful that no more attacks were planned for the foreseeable future. They wondered what would happen if there was nobody to stand up for them when they grow too old fight for themselves. The Suit should rest much easier now. The thug was due to leave the locality immediately. For the Introverts, distraction was the order of the night. Light entertainment would help fill the bar later, masking most of the vigilantes' sense of justice. Apparently, because no one lost an eye, this was acceptable.

Barry was cornered by the Leader and discreetly shown the disturbing mobile phone footage on mute. As the recording started, he realized why he was being shown it: he was now involved. Watching it made him an accessory after the fact in their eyes. He felt the need to reassess the character of his established clientele. As a protective measure, he refused to accept money for drinks from the posse all night. The Extroverts made no genuine attempts to do so. The Introverts sloped towards the sanctuary of the snug. Better to stay out of reach and physically separate themselves from locals who might bustle in through the door with the breaking news. Fearing their posture would betray their involvement, they sat together. Deflated silence would be enough to suggest their participation in the event. Introverts don't enjoy having to lie for the common good.

29

The Introverts began to think honestly. The attack was not a victory on behalf of the Suit but a weak response to their own fears. The Extroverts were still fuelled by their secret. They nudged each other and winked over large gulps of lager. It had been a while since they had felt approval from locals other than themselves, even if it was just the Introverts. The swell of inaccurate hearsay filled the bar. The Extroverts drew energy and empowerment from it, sniggering to conceal their possession of details. Their laughter would to be the loudest heard later on, the type of laughter that grated on guilty introverted nerves. In the silence of the confining, wood-panelled snug, the Introverts privately accepted that they had crossed a line. The enclosed space seemed confessional and conspiratorial at the same time. They whispered subtle reassurances to themselves that the Suit would benefit from their actions. Certain defences had to be enforced by offensive means sooner or later in life. They had been forced to fight. If they hadn't, they too might be victims someday. By choosing a side, they had sent a signal to miscreants that they were all on the same hymn sheet, whether they liked it or not. The snug council pondered on whether they should lie low until the inevitable rounds of gossip died down. The notion was rejected.

The Extroverts had remained bonded by praise for each other throughout the evening. They were all equals again as a result of their earlier act of bravado. Equals until alpha male instincts threw their weight behind a pretender to the throne once more. Tonight had a distinct start-from-scratch feeling to it. It was a leveller, one of those off-season moments when popularity, position, and equal status reminded all of the boom times. Barry remembered those busy nights when all his locals pitched in to ease the bottlenecks at the beer taps and collect empty glasses without being asked. There had to be a release for the Extroverts some time. It had been brewing for years, and it looked like they had an opportunity tonight. Barry did not seem his usual self, distant behind the counter. He deflected guilty thoughts. Had he incriminated himself simply by buying drinks for the posse?

Morty's was never brimming with people on a Sunday evening. All it took was an incident or scandal to bring people out for an update. Everybody that knew connected people drank there. This rural networking centre compiled accurate information faster than any other. The elderly felt comfortable there. Barry was considered a trusted, objective, and discreet information source for them. These good people might feel betrayed by him for straying from his usual neutral stand point and crossing a sinister line. The goodwill of the bar was threatened by tonight's event, and collecting empty pint glasses wouldn't clear his participation in it.

It didn't take much to fill the narrow doorway of the snug. Barry consumed it and stared at the remorseful faces within. The atmosphere suggested that all was not well with members of its back benches. Reaching in to collect their empty glasses and concentrating on his clutch of empties, he whispered something. Unified nods of appreciation came from the group, who pretended they understood his mumble. No one had lost an eye. They were lucky this time. That was the gist of it. One breaking voice whispered that they shouldn't get involved with this kind of shit anymore. Unified nods of agreement once more thanked Barry for hearing their communal guilt. They'd have to close the snug door from now on. It would restrict the impact of grief heading their way in the future.

Weaving through stationary punters, Barry made it back behind the bar with an armful of stacked empty glasses. Time to make a phone call to Dennis and find out if he had heard anything (accurate) concerning tonight's events. 'Dennis, Barry here, just a quick question ... Did you get any joy with the Sub? Ha ha, he slipped away again? No, I haven't seen him. Maybe he's gone to ground in a new pub? A pronounced finger to lips signalled to others that orders for beer were on hold momentarily. 'Have you seen the Suit? Don't think he visits out of town? Barry had to listen to some below-the-belt comment from Dennis and laughed awkwardly in the direction of the Elvis jumpsuit that was untangling wires from a mixing desk. The Ninja Paddy act would start soon.

People kept coming through the doors, anticipating more comic antics by Ninja Paddy. Setting up the DJ equipment and securing a microphone to its stand with masking tape were Ninja's ritual duties. Sound-check theatrics were embellished with fake Elvis tones and some irritating fingernail taps to interrupt the bass cacophony of the crowd. Then came a request for attention in a low, sombre voice. 'Ladies and gentlemen, a moment of your time please … Most of you are aware of the events that took place this evening. Scary times, my friends, scary times indeed, but I'd like to pay tribute to the elderly man that lived next door to the scene of that trouble.'

The Extroverts erupted, called out the Suit's name, and initiated a loud soccer chant that invaded the whole bar, gaining momentum to become a frenzied conga rhythm with lyrics that no one group could comfortably agree on before it thankfully withered away to allow Ninja to continue with his address. 'Now settle down, ladies and gentlemen, I would like to pay tribute to the Suit, a good man, a true gent. Most of you knew his corner over there and his polite, gentle voice-of-reason ways. But unfortunately, our elderly friend passed away in the early hours of this morning.'

A solitary pint glass broke on the snug floor. An American voice cursed respectfully. One Extrovert forcefully thumped the bar counter in frustration. The Introverts stared blankly at each other without exhaling, without making a sound or mustering up a blink.

'Also I'd like to pay tribute to you all in this bar because of the simple friendship and goodwill that you genuinely showed him. He'd thank you all for the part you all played in his last years. A life that sadly ended on his own. Thank you all for your attention.'

The bar was left mute by his words. Ninja wondered if he had overdone it. All in front of him stood still with what appeared to be suppressed anger and regret. He could not put his finger on their attachment to the Suit on this particular night. The Extroverts felt cheated. The Introverts felt worse about their involvement in an illegal activity. There was no victory. Somehow both sides felt that the thug had won. Barry picked up his mobile phone once again.

3

SUSPENSION

| | | |;|.|,|?|-|"""|()|

:

Two middle-aged Americans paused outside the front door of Hennessey's bar. An impressively designed promotional poster, at odds with their visual expectations, seemed to have caught their attention. It was time for Tom, the bar owner, to go for a cigarette break and act as information provider for the two curious tourists.

'Says on this poster that you got some guy called Ninja Paddy appearing tonight. Is that right? We're wondering if it's some rock band? Bet it gets really loud? How loud d'ya suppose it gets? Army damaged my hearing. Hurts like hell in the morning, and she can't stay out too late, y'know. Loud music,' said the male American.

Tom drew extra long on his cigarette, trying to conjure up an explanation. Heavy dollops of mystery and slow intrigue were added to his inhale as he sized up the pair. 'It's entertainment with a unique flavour. Believe me, you won't see the likes of it replicated elsewhere in the country. Years of martial arts training in the Orient: ju-jitsu, karate, judo mixed with the dance moves of contemporary hip-hop and the cinematic references of popular action movies thrown in,' said Tom. He spoke with such a sinister air of hushed disbelief that the curious couple felt like they were secretly being warned to stay far away. This might be something they were not supposed to understand.

'Holy shit, do we need to book in advance or something?'

'I'm Irene and this is my husband, Glenn,' said the female.

Scrutinising his cigarette, Tom summarily condemned it with a last draw and casually flicked it to the ground for shoe-leather execution. 'The last time that Ninja Paddy played, we had the doors locked at ten o'clock for safety. Jam-packed inside were people from all over, had to make room for the journalists and TV crews.'

Dumbstruck, the two tourists faced each other at once. This chaos sounded great to them. They'd better get themselves back to the hotel and freshen up. Maybe they should bring the camera?

'Absolutely no flash photography allowed, sir! He's … How should I say this best? He's a total professional,' Tom said and casually kicked his cigarette butt from the pavement as punctuation.

Both Americans agreed this was better than some half-hearted guided tour. With a certain sadness, Irene and Glenn accepted foregoing photographic proof, just to witness the Ninja Paddy spectacle. No visual evidence to bring back to their homeland and prove that they had seen this local legend. Tom beckoned another barman to the front door, where he was shown the latest tourists to fall for the Ninja myth. The pair of American ambassadors ambled down the street with rotating waistband pouches, waving at passers-by, who cautiously waved back with woolly smiles. Don't embarrass the tourists too much and the locals will entertain them later was Tom's lesson for today. He had become an extremely competent and highly believable mic controller over time. The DJ was an integral part in the Ninja Paddy experience. Each week two new guests, dressed head-to-toe in black (the Ninja Stars), would happily assist Ninja Paddy. This act was well-known locally, and everyone liked to guess who the Ninja Stars were. Ninja made the effort to give the locals value for their money. Seducing the odd celebrity to show up and participate in his cause was difficult. This micro-circus toured three bars in town throughout the month. Usually Ninja performed on Friday and Sunday evenings because he worked in the bar most other days.

Originally this performance was born out of boredom caused by the economic crash, but it eventually became a vehicle for any local cause that he felt was worth helping. It took some time to get people on-board. Nobody gave to charities anymore, not without reservation. So many people had been ripped off by legit organisations in the past. People didn't seem to give as much money unless there was something in it for them. The recessions of the past didn't help his charitable cause much either. Society didn't want just to contribute; it wanted to look fabulous for doing so. Ninja reckoned he'd entertain for his charitable supper instead. Give the people something out of the ordinary, make a real comic effort. Make people laugh before you ask for their money, and maybe they'd feel good about giving to your cause.

'Tonight, we have the same deal as with most of our Ninja Paddy shows this year. The proceeds will provide assistance to Meals on Wheels.' Tom, as emcee, briefly summarised the plight of the rural elderly and Ninja's mission to help them out every Sunday. He made it all sound as if Ninja were a time traveller or an exotic Arctic explorer. Every week this introduction was embellished to keep from becoming repetitive. The Sunday Meals on Wheels' service was one activity that Ninja was doing without any help. Showing up for a performance made locals feel they were lending a hand without getting either one dirty. His act removed the need for effort from many begrudging minds.

Ninja had been working on this performance for weeks. It needed meticulous detailing. Martial arts and hip-hop choreography took up most of his time, more than the grand finale. In fairness to Ninja, he did learn a few unorthodox moves and possessed a natural sense of rhythm. But it was the stupidity between moves that cracked everyone up. He nailed the failed 'look into my eyes' Vegas magician stage presence. The DJ had seamless skills, hitting switches furiously in anticipation of his master's off-script changes. The music ranged from Japanese garden music to old school hip-hop. Any attempts by the Ninja Stars to dance were strictly spontaneous.

According to Tom, Ninja had defied both science and logic in his creation. This may raise questions about the sanity and well-being of its creator. Tom wanted to praise DJ Grass Dropper and exaggerated a dismayed reaction to Ninja, who was shaking his head profusely from a poorly lit corner behind him. Drum and bass beats launched into wild karate kicks. Some one-inch punches failed to shatter aeroboard panels held by the Ninja Stars. Behind a black balaclava, a Ninja Star laughed each time Irene loudly asked if those guys were for real. Next, a flurry of fist rolls, up close and personal, to freak out the more nervous front-row bystanders. Tom rushed to introduce Ninja Paddy and his motley crew to much hilarity. It was one of Ninja's best entrances. Not that his earlier attempts were supposed to be taken seriously in any way.

Ninja's main event was to jump a table of toy buses and trucks with a kid's big wheel bike. He managed this while wearing his white Ninja Knievel jumpsuit and cape. He solemnly made it known that if anything went wrong, he was to be buried wearing it. The Ninja Stars for that night's performance were beefed up especially for Ninja's safety. The local rugby team had generously provided two of its largest team members. Both sportsmen said they were happy to help out as long as they didn't have to pole dance or strip from the waist down. After noticing the two Americans in the audience, Ninja saw an opportunity for an unexpected twist to the finale. He would clear a prostrate male American, head to toe, with his big wheel bike. When opportunity for unexpected comedy presented itself, it would be used to vary his weekly performance.

'This DJ endeavours to introduce you all to the rogue talent, nay, reckless heights of madness that his master has yet to achieve,' roared Tom. He took a sip of water, desperately trying to clear his hoarse throat in order to command a dramatic pause. Then he stressed his vocal chords further to impart that he had already pleaded with Ninja not to perform this daring feat tonight for fear of injury and because he had nobody to clear up the bar afterwards. 'Ladies and Gentlemen, tonight's challenge will require the assistance of a brave volunteer. Someone who isn't from Ireland, for a change? The crowd sensed a twist. A wandering spotlight caught Glenn's doe-eyed wonder in its beam. You, Sir! it clearly suggested.

Up marched the smiling victim representing a nation far away. The locals erupted with applause. Unsure of what to expect, Glenn chatted to Tom about his travels and punched the air every time the crowd cheered for him. In the background, two small ramps were being placed in the middle of the floor, roughly seven feet apart. Ninja, deep in concentration, measured the gap heel to toe. Ramps were tested for safety. He was ready. He nodded to the Ninja Stars. They nodded back in their black stealth suits and grabbed Glenn firmly by each arm, guiding him to lie between the ramps. The lights dimmed, and the roar of a motorcycle rattled through the speakers.

The faces of the locals lit up with embarrassed grins for an anxious Glenn. Ninja was engulfed by handheld spotlight, making the blacked-out Ninja Stars invisible. Ninja pedalled furiously and propelled the big-wheel tricycle towards the ramp to the accompaniment of engine noise. He hit the ramp with extreme care, allowing both Ninja Stars to hoist him awkwardly into the air. Camera flashes provoked a pronounced New York accent to complain about the lapse in the photography policy. Ninja waved his hands in regal gestures until calling a halt halfway across to much laughter. Held in suspension, Ninja saluted the paralysed American before descending gracefully to frenzied applause and whistles.

A performance that lasted less than ten minutes catapulted the spectators into a warm, comfortable humour for the rest of the evening and raised €147. Two large Ninja Stars hovered over Ninja, trying to control their boyish tittering and shushing themselves with aggressive wrist slaps before taking costumed selfies, with flash, on their phones. This elicited the desired 'No flash photography, my ass' response from the only disgruntled female. Ninja knew that it was time to explain to Irene what was going on before she took it too seriously. Still in his Elvis/Knievel attire, he informed them both with a straight face. Glenn was never in any real danger, he stressed.

Irene was impressed. Ninja realised that there was no way that the next bar would raise the same amount of money without the two of them participating. He wondered if they'd consider joining him and his charity circus and pretend to be oblivious to what was going on. Bring the camera too? They battled each other to agree with wide-eyed glee. He figured that if both had known the full details, they would not have freaked out so brilliantly. At least now they could have the comfort of knowing it was all for a good cause. There was an issue concerning Glenn's motivation. He had to have an exit plan for everything. He had risk issues and needed some clarification on his exact role in the next charade. Irene teased him and wanted to know if Glenn should bring a change of underwear, just in case.

TO BE PART

OF SOMETHING,

MORE IMPORTANTLY,

GLENN WAS CAUGHT OFF-GUARD.

TO BE ASKED TO BE PART

IRENE DIDN'T NEED TO BE ASKED TWICE.

OF SOMETHING

WAS TRULY

AN HONOUR

THESE DAYS.

The two newest members of Ninja Paddy's undercover troop went down a treat with the other two bars, convincing spectators that they thought the spectacle was completely legit. Glenn would remark loudly that the Ninja Stars needed to start taking their jobs seriously, Goddammit. Ninja's life was in their hands. True to plan, flash photography was provided, and, without prompting, the Americans would exclaim after every burst of light, 'Hey guys, no flash photography. He's gonna lose his shit for real!' As the drama continued Irene adapted this to, 'Is this shit for real?' A full night raised close to €400 for the local charity.

At the close of each performance, Ninja pointed out that the American couple were indeed planted, just to enhance the overall amusement. Both tourists received a warm wolf-whistle of appreciation from onlookers. This evening made them feel slightly embarrassed initially, but they were happy they'd taken part. They kept looking intensely at each other, trying to remember any experience remotely like this one. Glenn's stint in the army had been conservative compared to everything he witnessed tonight. Back home they were just faces in the crowd, spectators, but never really participants in social events. It was good to be part of something worthwhile. The couple had their tourist status upgraded in their own eyes and the eyes of others. Everyone's facial expressions were broad and sincere.

The next day Ninja had to work for Dennis in Maguire's. He would be in at nine every Monday morning and finish up at three o'clock in the afternoon. The early stocktaking would be easy enough. The Players would be in situ, as usual, along with a few punters from the bookies next door. Sipping away on pints and quietly chasing cryptic clues in the racing pages to place a small bet and win big money. These guys were never troublesome, whether their horse won or not. They helped him relax while he reconstructed his weekend performance. His recent performances had come dangerously close to failure. Too frequent lately. Last night he was rescued by the randomness of two American tourists. How close was that?

The Bookie Bunch scanned all the dead print headlines of sporting taunts, paradise wins, and close-but-no-cigar misfortunes. At the end of the bar, the Players occupied another world, one of their own importance. This group had no time to get involved with Ninja's unfolding sense of self-doubt. Requests were usually limited to a pint and the odd, will'ya mind'm'seat request when the riddle of the racing saddle had been solved. Minutes later they'd slide back in through the front door with that familiar shoulder-sideways grace that had evolved from a lifetime of being late for class. What made them this way? Some were slightly older than others, all focused, with fortune teller chin strokes and some irrational good luck. Each member would zone into their predictable routine. These ritually rigid ways had always unsettled Ninja. The idea of treading water through life did not appeal to him, but that was where he seemed to be heading. His stage act was definitely nearing an end.

Ninja's brand of entertainment was strategically, but never systematically, planned. His crowd-pleasing relied on sensing the mood at each venue for any potential awkwardness. Appearance, age, and fashion informed him of what to expect. Check the temperament of the staff, know historic faction fights, gauge the body language of the most confident locals, like the Players, and beware of forced, highly dramatic laughter.

Ninja broke away from his thoughts to finish pulling a slow pint and then returned to his mental critique. He had added to his list of observations lately. Address nervous gigglers individually. Always imply the need for a volunteer as a threat to the audience. A nervous giggler could empower the confident locals. Check out if any local tragedy had taken place recently; messy hecklers always had deep issues they'd like to vent. Command attention assertively if lack of interest devolves into background chatter. Always compliment good-looking women with a sense of genuine respect and quickly stare their partner into submission. Keep a good eye on the sad and the withdrawn faces, and see if they lighten up or smirk uncontrollably. Then you'll know if you are on the right track.

The more Ninja thought about his comic act, the more impressed he became with his intuitive treatment of previous audiences. The three bar venues proved tougher to entertain these days, tougher to extract that tommy-gun laughter. The limitations of a small town circuit and its familiarity with his sense of humour reduced his appeal. He craved the type of comedy that begged the crowd to search themselves for reasons they didn't see the joke coming in the first place. There were some that would never get his humour. Ninja Paddy, as an act, had been a breath of fresh air once, but his tank of humour was running out of gas.

Who else would risk being ridiculed by people he knew by name? We're too sophisticated for failure these days. Fear of failure was the main reason he enjoyed the British comedian Tommy Cooper, the only comic performer that Ninja knew of whose actual death on stage got as much laughter as his comedic death on stage. Today's adults needed to lighten up, get embarrassed more often.

The key to great comedy (with his audience) was that he alone must be prepared to take the ridicule bullet for them. Absorb their insecurities and then project them straight back at them at speed. All in the knowledge that they, the audience, have the licence and blessing of those around them, to confidently laugh out loud.

A change was needed; Ninja needed to take stock. He was not in tune with the next generation, but he didn't see the necessity of trying to analyse Generation Z or C. Could he end up like one of these predictable people in front of him now? They didn't deviate from their personal preferences. There was no give with these people. They weren't great at taking advice, and they heeded no orders or criticism. If something unwelcome entered their routine, it could ruin their day immediately. One minute they were like a stone that couldn't be read, and the next, they turned into a monolith of tight-lipped crankiness. A heavy sigh trailed behind one of the Bookie Bunch as he ghosted back through the bar door. A warning to others that there was potential grief to follow. Ninja felt the need to start polishing glasses.

'I wouldn't bother going next door to place a bet for a few minutes. The Sub is just after showing his smarmy face,' said the annoyed punter. The messenger was not usually the type to open his mouth unless to warn his brothers of the Bookie Bunch. He'd get no response until he had returned to the company of his neglected pint. Everyone knew that the Sub had not been barred from Maguire's yet. There had been rumours linking him to some funny money. The pest's presence next door disrupted the concentration needed for picking horses, like sheep worried by the threat of a wolf. Would he still be at the bookie counter when they wanted to place their bet? The Sub never heeded their requests to get lost.

Ninja had worked for Maguire's bar on and off for over fifteen years. It had served him well. The owner, Dennis Maguire, allowed him to make his own judgement calls on barring people and rarely questioned his reasons for taking action. Hearing the Players mention that the Sub was involved in passing dodgy notes caught his attention. One customer said he was present when Barry from Morty's rang. He relayed the basic story to Ninja, and it had impressed him. It was a scheme that certainly had a bit of grey matter in it and was daring in its execution. The bar collective shrugged in unison. The last time that any one of them took responsibility for anything in their lives (other than themselves) was difficult to remember. A quick phone call to Barry for accuracy on local matters but especially when the Sub was involved.

'Who will I say I am for a laugh?' he asked the Players. Hand cupped on receiver, he waited. 'Useless, ye … oh is that you, Barry? Ninja here, have you a second to talk? Good, the boys here were telling me about the dodgy €20 y'slipped the Sub.'

The hysterical laughter at the other end of the phone was a mixture of loud voices coming from patrons who had figured out that Barry was trying to talk about the Sub attack. Ninja tried to interrupt the crossfire on Barry's end of the phone by asking the name of the mastermind who tricked the Sub. He was left listening to an unattended phone.

Barry rang Ninja back and tried to build a better profile of the new trickster in town, the Aloof. The reason nobody knew him was that he used to drink underage elsewhere. This young enigma was now of age and had completed a year in college, but his father had lost his business and was now leasing Larry's shop. All above board. No history of bad blood between the kid and the Sub. He was just looking out for the Suit. Barry had loud customers to serve and was about to hang up when Ninja remembered to ask if any details had been released concerning the death of the Suit. 'Barry?' The call ended abruptly. He must be busy, Ninja assumed.

The bar customers took little notice of the phone call's abrupt ending as they were too concerned with the Sub's appearance next door. 'Y'miserable bunch of wasters. Who's working next door? Margaret?' Ninja asked for a betting slip and dialled the phone number with the bravery of a kid forging a sick note for a truant classmate. 'Hello there, Margaret, Ninja here next door. Would you please alert all of your customers that there seems to be a number of dodgy notes flying around and that all transactions, especially those involving twenties, need to be thoroughly vetted?'

Margaret immediately relayed his information to all in the bookies. Ninja heard her loud and clear. He waved frantically at the Bookie Bunch, telling them to turn around in their seats quickly. He pointed to the main window and the group rotated slowly to look outside. The inside of Maguire's front window was not a discreet place to be seen. It meant one of two things: you were either gambling or avoiding work responsibilities. There they were, all watching the Sub outside in a state of suppressed panic.

Ninja peeped through the available space between the shoulders and necks of the observers. They spotted the Sub. 'There's a man on borrowed time, lads. There's nowhere for him to go. All his excuses have been exhausted; all trust in him gone, disappeared long ago. He'll tell lies to the priest on his deathbed,' said Ninja.

They all turned away from the window in unison to ponder on the likelihood of this latest bar stool prophecy ever happening.

4

PASSENGERS

| | | | |.|,|?|-|""|0|

;

According to Bart, he was responsible for killing a man sixty years ago. The statement stunned Glenn and Irene into silence, though the words were spoken with genuine regret. The pensioner was in mid-ramble when they stepped through the front door. Bart's facial expression, his only one, stayed fixed. Poke his eye and it would bleed tears like sand from a holey sack. Both Americans looked in disbelief at their first face-to-face dealing with the elderly in rural isolation. Ninja marched towards the kitchen table with a hot tinfoil-covered plate. 'Sunday again. I got you your favourites, Bart: two packs of digestives. Don't eat them all at once, y'greedy bastard, or you'll be stuck on the toilet for days. Remember the last time? I know you don't like the new lady doctor getting to see all your bits. I see you're cleaning up after yourself. Good man. Keeps the flies and our little rodent friends from paying us a visit. Do you want salt for your potatoes, and what have we here? Very flash, Bart, cranberry sauce. Were you in town this week? Margaret dropped by, then. You need good neighbours. She's a peach. Heart of gold. Have you any letters for posting? You know how your lot worry; they can't be around much, but you know that. Be good and drop them a letter to let them know how you are, will you? Found this old photo. You're a great memory man for the faces, but tell me who's this handsome devil in the middle? Will you look who it is? Jesus, y'cut a sharp frame at the dance hall! Half of that crew are gone now. You always had the health, though. Do you want this at the table and eat it while its nice and hot, or do you want it over there? Over there it is then; we'll just get you a tea towel and some cutlery. Brought you some milk if you'd like a small glass. Is there anything you need brought from the shed or anything before we feck off, Bart? I could drop you into town later and Margaret could bring you home,' said Ninja. The pensioner heard every word but his eyes never left Irene.

Ninja moved the American pair towards the door, quietly informing them that the only one dead was Bart himself. No murder mystery in the old house, just a mind playing tricks on a man who had endured too much, too young.

Ninja was one heavily layered individual. Irene accepted that some people she had encountered over the years were difficult to read. He was one. Every farmhouse gate they crossed that day transformed their new friend into a totally different person. She wondered if he could be that adept at dealing with one poor unfortunate after another without incurring psychological side effects. She had never met a chameleon as crazy as this Irishman before. Each rural householder was treated with a different form of humanity.

The van snaked and rattled around camouflaged tracks aggressively. A thought suddenly struck Glenn. 'There has to be another word that you guys can use instead of road?' His honesty made Ninja laugh out loud. Irene examined her fingernails for damage. She jokingly congratulated Ninja for having such a clean dashboard. She knew nothing could remain on it safely, not with these 'roads' and not at this speed. His driving style on overgrown, uncharted trails was never mentioned once on their itinerary. Shoulders swayed around tight corners, and suspension-spanking potholes every twenty feet caused their conversation to break frequently. It recommenced whenever they reached the security of an unfinished patch of County Council tarmac.

The unforeseen effort of the day had truly humbled the two passengers. Whenever one of these rural missions became difficult, it motivated Ninja to push his stage act further. He'd have to leave each old soul alone for a week to battle their fears. Bart's situation, like many others, could not be resolved without proper care. An old man left in isolation, nearing the end of his life cycle, becomes a silent affair with himself and no other. Besides appearing to be borderline crazy, Bart was regressing and lately had started to revisit earlier parts of his life. Relying on the constructed memories of others seemed pointless to him, especially when very few people knew or tried to understand the concept of being Bart.

All his earlier decisions in life had been forced under the carpet. Visits from his kids grew less frequent, trickling down to an occasional rehearsed phone call from somewhere far from here.

Irene wondered if her own life could have meant something more. She could end up just like one of those poor unfortunates, as Ninja called them. Not like the rurally isolated but forgotten in a small apartment, never knowing her neighbours. There were no Ninjas in New York to pay her a welcome visit. Glenn was getting older by the minute and was destined to die long before her. If it happened the other way around and she went first, their home would be a wreck. Her man was incapable of boiling an egg. Mortality sucks when you have to face the fact that life ends in death. She could handle a world without Glenn; his core had long been depleted.

The van continued to take charge of the designated route, sniffing its way through a fading historical landscape and Ninja's dubious word-of-mouth mythology. No mysterious Midwestern American place names like Dead Man's Gully here, only O'Brien's Bridge or Flanagan's Hill to tease the tourists with flatline intrigue. This secret world passed by the tourists quicker than they would have liked. Ninja had an annoying habit of mentioning location names after they had passed beyond sight. His guests' curiosity made their necks crane backwards to catch a glimpse. This high-speed journey through unpredictable countryside had become a test of memory rather than the traditional notion of sight-seeing. Ninja reckoned Irene and Glenn would probably need hypnosis or some form of regression therapy on their return to the States just to remember their visit.

The journey eventually took its toll on all three. The cocoon of the van cabin had become devoid of banter. Each was now privy to the brushed-aside aspects of Irish tourism, witnesses to the reality of ageism and neglect in the wake of a modern Ireland trying to find its feet. Each would have to individually dust off the residue of the day's activity in his or her own way, justifying doing so with the belief that they were good people with good intentions in the midst of popular complacency. The bubbly voice of the local radio DJ was quashed by push-button dismissal. They would ride back to town in slow conversation with no pothole warnings from Ninja.

Vacant stares betrayed their conscious interpretations of the rustic rehab they had visited today. Irene and Glenn would leave the complexities of dealing with the elderly to Ninja, and pay him the respect he deserved. Irene scrambled around in her bag for a pen. Ninja's mobile phone interrupted her search, its ringtone fixing her attention. His dreadful techno ringtone could not be taken seriously. She was usually suspicious of anyone over forty who had a ringtone that was at odds with their public personality. She could accept that Ninja might be going through some sort of midlife crisis or was just oblivious to his consumerism bracket. Irene hoped that marketing, manufactured consent, hadn't fooled Ninja. She reached out for the phone and read out the caller details. It said, BOTHER. Ninja nodded to accept, and she held the phone to his ear while he continued to drive. This simple act felt odd. Irene hardly knew Ninja, and it seemed slightly weird to be depended on by people other than her long-standing husband. Focused and serious, the call was taken on a savage stretch of road for added effect. Both Americans realised that Ninja lived by a different set of safety rules.

The worst section of road must have anticipated the phone call out of mischief. Chassis slapped, cabin cracked, suspension smacked the underneath of their rigid cab seats with unforgiving brutality. All this volatile driving had knocked an abnormal falsetto scream out of Glenn. Irene cried with her face covered.

Random surges of acceleration, clutch-pops with violent side-swiped synchronicity made all three voyagers laugh hard. This white-water road rafting was the most excitement the two Americans had experienced in years. Ninja exaggerated his driving style to prolong the fun. Glenn looked uncomfortable and may have loosened a kidney. He asked to stop the van before his bladder cut loose. Ninja pulled over promptly. He made comments questioning Glenn's diet and advising him to keep an eye on the porter and the underwear department. Ninja used his comic timing to bring Irene close to tears with laughter. The image of Glenn's shoulder sighs as he relieved himself filled her side mirror with comic relief.

Irene finally reined in her laughter to a canter and could speak without collapsing in a hysterical heap. Glenn could be a while yet, so she inspected a van manual after rummaging in the glove compartment. Ninja was transfixed by the consequences of having to return the phone call that had been aborted. His mask had dropped momentarily. Irene asked if it was serious. He snapped out of staring at his phone and laughed. Everything was serious with his brother. Bother was too damned serious. Washing socks was serious to him, he claimed. There were no indications in his text message that there was anything more than his brother's usual concern. Ninja proceeded to tap out his message. His text replies were exact, short, and lean, but could be slow in returning.

His brother was never one to contact Ninja unless he was on his way to the family house or had already booked into the hotel on arrival. He never let anyone know exactly when he would arrive in town or why. International man of mystery. Neither brother bothered communicating much because they were from different worlds. No offence intended and none taken. Knowing his brother would book a hotel room, he assumed that he could meet with him for a pint or two when he cleaned up after dropping the Americans off. Ninja could meet his brother later for a drink at the hotel.

Having successfully completed his task, Glenn removed all driving debris from the front grill before getting back into the van. Ninja thanked him and said he'd take care of the rest when he made it home. Glenn reckoned that no sane New Yorker would believe what they'd seen today. They went straight back into first gear, high revs, jump-clutch, and buckaroo lurches from the van, which played an integral part in the humour for the day. Narrow roads began to widen, assuring them that the safety of home base was within reach and relaxation would be in their grasp. These initially quaint roads gave other motorists the impression that the back roads were not really too bad. Back roads brought out the jackass in Ninja's driving because he knew them so well, safe in the knowledge that there was little or no traffic on them.

H U M O U R
P R O V I D E D

}

a brief glimpse of the escapism

harboured by all three and began

to reveal itself.

{

A W K W A R D

SILENCE USHERED IT AWAY

BEFORE A BOND BETWEEN

THEM TOOK HOLD.

Within sight of town, the radio received a reluctant pardon and was switched on again. Conversation had withered away. Two fading faces focused on the hotel entrance as the van pulled to an abrupt halt. 'I was just wondering if the two of ye would be interested in going for one before I headed off home?' Ninja asked innocently.

The question rattled Glenn's exhausted mind to a state of frozen awe until Ninja clarified that he meant a pint and nothing sordid. He had to politely explain to Glenn that this was definitely a no-swingers motel. Irene was taken aback. Split-second images were pushed away from her mind by everything that was decent about Glenn, and she blurted out a laugh. The reality of today's journey was going to be washed, dried, and placed on a shelf of experience.

The van sped away, muck-wheeled and much emptier. It was easier for Ninja to think, now that the two Americans had been released from the van. He had definitely made an impact on his passengers by showing them his version of rural Ireland, the version on the fringes, protected from tourist traps by less than welcoming tracks. He had Irene's support. Sometimes the Irish needed to be embarrassed by outsiders before natives would offer support locally. Tourists that spent time there and liked it were quickly forgotten. Those that pointed out their failings were indulged. Ninja hoped that Glenn and Irene would talk about their observations to others tonight without dreading their drive to the airport the next day.

The van exterior needed an immediate hose down, a chore that would help Ninja relax before he faced the night ahead. Years of learning to separate the various expectations that he allowed others to invest in him were not really paying off. Helping others by making a fool of himself was not going to work out in the long run. Never mind the responsibility required to handle family and bar work at the same time. Hard graft required mental discipline, but time for reflection was becoming a necessity. Stepping down might ignite the efforts of others, and hopefully the torch would be accepted by another. It was about time he found a potential heir to his Sunday throne.

The van showed signs of distress, scratches from gateways that seemed to shift and tighten a little bit more each Sunday. The mechanical wonder worked hard on behalf of those isolated dependents. Keeping its best side out all day was wearing the van's grilled smile thin. It, too, got tired lately. The workhorse was having its own form of mechanical midlife crisis. Couldn't quite do what it used to but still thought it could. From a distance, it maintained the appearance of being capable. A mute, metal cocoon for Ninja's monologues and wishes. If the van started to fall apart, he'd have to call a stop to the Sunday run for sure.

The wheels were coming loose around Ninja, and soon it would be time for him to ask for assistance from the only family member he could. His father's ability to give advice had become another casualty of old age, similar to many of the people he had visited that day. Parking the van at home, he never knew what would greet him. It made him approach the driveway and the front door with caution. So far, his father had remained indoors, but who could say for how long? His son feared that someday he'd return from the Sunday run to find his father wandering outdoors in his pyjamas, dazed, and confused. Ninja was never afraid of making a holy show of himself, but there was no way he would allow his father to be a source of ridicule to others.

As he left the van to cool down on the driveway, his ears pricked. The static sound of a half-tuned radio greeted him. His father was going deaf. Ninja found the front door ajar and his father sitting two feet from the TV screen. There was no knowing what mishap would greet him these days: a tap running full on, an abandoned Hoover left whining in the hallway. Usually his father sat perched in front of some mind-numbing television programme. If you asked him what he was watching, he couldn't remember why he had been sitting there. These were the little things that worried him most while he was out in the van. The old man had lived clean and lean with everything in its place, but soon safety issues would have to outrank his father's independence.

'Keep your house clean and don't be picking at it,' he'd say … a lot. The shell of his father had a confused soul housed within it now. The idea of being absent at the moment that this soul decided to depart worried Ninja. He could be driving around the rural back roads to take care of a few strangers when all that the old man knew, the here and now in rational terms, decided to wander from its origins? When the validity of backlogged short-term memories and long-term secrets separated, leaving Ninja to tie them all back together again. There must be so much within that man that never got to be heard. He only ever confided in their mother, always out of earshot and out of the way. God forbid that any demons come out to play. All that his sons knew of him was good. Both preferred it stayed that way.

Ninja's concern was never in question, and his older brother wouldn't require hard proof, but he would have to provide several examples of his father's behaviour to allow his sibling to form a clearer picture. His brother could gauge the severity of the situation and possibly take appropriate action later. The picture that he formed was of a reserved old man who may have developed a flaw in the safety mechanism that protected his inner thoughts and memories. It was impossible for either son to anticipate what could be unleashed. Beware the quiet ones. Whatever had started to mess with their father's perception of reality was taking a firm farmer's grip on Ninja's darkest intuitive fears. Would his father harm himself unwittingly while there was nobody to prevent it?

No point in trying to figure it all out when there might be no solution but care. Time to face the fact that he now slept under the same roof with a replica of the person he knew as dad. None of this was material for strangers, too many long and awkward pauses, too few articulate words to explain. This was, without doubt, a face-to-face job for family members only. No dramatic emphasis. Ninja knew that whatever it took, whatever aspects of their lives needed to be altered would be done without irrational conditions or petty resistance Once both brothers accepted the new reality, preparation for their father's departure would take care of itself.

A quick hose to the wheel muck before it dried. Windscreen wipers waved off soapy water like a kid shaking off parental attempts to clean his face in front of peers. Ninja never let dirt build up from week to week. One day he'd just give in and pick at it, letting it fall to rust.

The van was cleared of its contents, and the external cleaning was finished without much grief. Then a shower for himself before his meeting in town. Might it be better to walk the stress of the day off? He decided to drive because the walk would surely sap whatever energy he had left. The American experience had worn him out and could affect his performance later on. His brother was probably already in town, unpacked and relaxing at the hotel.

The shower rinsed the activity of his day away. Five years of the Sunday run had made him question why he should care for these few rural remnants. Stick your neck out too far and everyone will let you hang yourself. Thoughts like these were growing more frequent, niggling at him before he prepared for every Sunday morning journey. Take a month off, a few weeks away from keeping the best side out. He needed to take a break from listening to the same five-minute conversations every Sunday, no disrespect to the elderly. Thoughts of being able to stop and sleep guilt-free had been chipping away in a region of his consciousness. These thoughts might slip out unintentionally. If asked, he would have to be honest and admit he'd had enough of the Sunday run.

There was no chance of burnout with his brother; he dealt with stress differently. He addressed issues head on. The big problems could be delegated, and if the small ones needed tinkering, he'd just take out his large toolkit of experience. Ninja knew when something was wrong with a rural dweller. They will let you know politely. City people, according to the experience of his brother, bottled problems up and released each one with a slow fuse before anyone realised there was a problem. Nobody had family problems in the city, or they refused to admit to the emotional pressure that the city placed on its inhabitants. Ninja could never live there because nobody was who they claimed to be.

The if concerning the end of the Sunday run was rapidly changing to when. Either way it signalled the death of Ninja Paddy, the entertainer. One necessity had been born directly from the other. Without the charity aspect of the pub performances, it would be difficult to justify his stage antics. He would have to put an end to both. Later this week he would annoy his graphic designer on how best to retire the Ninja brand in style. His friend loved a design challenge. It would be interesting to see his face when he got total creative control again. According to his creative friend the number of clients that allowed him total creative freedom, were rarer than hen's teeth these days. Better save up some of the money for the last Ninja promotion. A shower and fresh clothes reduced the stress, making the drive to meet his brother a welcome break. A retirement gig would not be mentioned until later, if at all. He'd keep quiet in case he was misunderstood. The Sunday run had sapped civility from his shoulders and humour from his high cheek bones. Defences were running low, but he knew that he had enough energy to listen and reply honestly to questions concerning their father. Money wouldn't be an issue concerning his care. Time to put priorities in their correct order and fall in line with his elder's views. The evening would prove which sibling had looked furthest down the road of consequence. Common sense would demand to find a plan of action tonight.

Sedate Sunday evening streets and day-of-rest pavements provided ample parking space for Ninja's van. Gliding to a slow halt, the van slipped into view from the hotel bay window. His brother's recognisable frame was seated comfortably with a daily newspaper, hands high and ready to change the pages. If Ninja sat in the van and waited for his brother to return the observation, it would be nightfall. Their powers of concentration were equally strong, but they were used to using different parts of their brains. The side view mirror filled with the sight of the Sub drifting across the street towards Hennessey's. In the hotel window his brother watched Ninja shaking his head with disbelief at the Sub's arrogance.

CHAPTER

5

SOON

| | | | | |,|?|-|""|0|

Recently, Miss noticed her husband's increasing need to visit his father in the West, which left her to her own devices in the privacy of their secure Dublin home. Nobody would rush to her assistance if she were to have a heart attack while he was away on family business. It still functioned as a home and hadn't reached the status of glorified holding cell yet. Residing here for several years was no guarantee that her neighbours' names or their professional status were actually known. The couple had worked together since he had started the business but had decided to take a break recently. Two years ago, to be exact. The title of 'sit at home wife' never appeared on her list of goals before she decided to marry, and looking good on paper was not what she had intended for her future years. There was so much more to her than this.

Morning temperatures rose to toast the paper-thin canopy of cloud, instructing it to disperse. All signs pointed to having an early walk in the park now that he was away. Tourists would be easy to spot as they explored a city that once amazed her. She had arrived here as a rural tourist back in her teens. Day trips to Dublin had been her opportunity to let loose, trips that told her parents that they had better start keeping an eye on their daughter's new fella. He had not yet won their approval back then. That all changed when he got into college, and it appeared that his future was bright. She remembered day trips up from the country, drinking in the park, and her future husband sobering her up on the train home. Those previously lucid teen memories were beginning to lose their accuracy lately. Maybe her commitment to them was finally loosening. An energetic walk through the park would start her day afresh. Today was not a day to be wasted on emotional clutter. Her husband made it clear that he would not dare disturb her. He was not going to return from his family until she contacted him with an answer to his request to patch things up. She had been party to mutual neglect for the last few years. It might be time for her to admit to her role in the play. This honesty would cut the meanness out and leave some scope for a solution.

From a comfortable distance, the luminous vests of Gardaí signalled that there would be no entry through the park gates today. One Garda motorcycle flashed its lights dutifully and indicated that feeding the ducks would have to be placed on hold. Curiosity made her strain her neck, giving her a distinct busybody appearance. She continued to walk towards a group of people who seemed to be spectating. Sidestepping the intrigued onlookers, she realised that this was as close to an accident or crime scene as she'd ever been. Too much time tucked away from the reality of city strife. Walking towards her, looking as if he'd had his insensitive expectations quashed, was a pedestrian who had just withdrawn from the scene.

'Excuse me, Sir! I'm sorry, I don't mean to keep you from your business, but do you know what's going on in the park?' Her tone of voice showed no sign of insincerity. After a calculated pause to search for some economical words, the pedestrian obliged.

'A body. Homeless guy. Probably drugs,' he replied with the no-nonsense delivery of the bored, one used to remembering a condensed shopping list but not its true importance. His matter-of-fact manner caught her off guard and left her momentarily puzzled.

The informant continued on his walk without showing any noticeable signs of concern for the corpse in the park. The sun intervened and broke through her solemn thoughts, trying in vain to encourage her face to warm to a smile. Anxiety put brakes on her initial bravery but not her curiosity. Purposely slowing her walk to give the appearance of a relaxed stroller, she neared the guarded park entrance. A motorcycle sentry with a luminous jacket and white crash helmet raised a leather gloved hand. She deciphered a 'Nothing to see here, Ma'am' from his mumble. Before she had any ideas of peeking over his shoulder, an ambulance exited respectfully through the gates. No siren, no lights ablaze, and no apologies. Saluting in silence and restraining its horsepower, it rolled away. If she had left the house later, would she have assumed that it was a murder or an overdose? Social neglect was something that she associated with life in rural areas.

The shopping centre by the park showed no signs that it had been adversely affected by the death. Commerce never missed a beat. No minute's silence from its cash register drawers. No one expected the city to shut down just for the sake of …? The city never knew the dead man by name. It had always dealt with this type of death differently. It never dwelt on the dead unless it was a major media personality or of historical interest. Down in the country, in her home town, everyone would have been in mourning, probably more so than ever if they didn't even know the victim's name. Small towns picked over death in far greater detail. It gave grieving a greater chance. It was personal. Every local sang from the same hymn sheet when it came to death.

No amount of planning could have prepared her for a random death in the park, not that she had any specific plan for her walk in the first place. Move along, avoid the spectacle, and enjoy the warmth of the sunshine without being bullied by weekday traffic or the silent menace of cycle couriers. Getting lost in her favourite bookshop was always an option. The last few years had made her sit at home and sprawl, reading far more than her bookshelves would suggest. She developed a world of questioning and concern unknown to her husband. He only half listened to what she said at home. A polite 'aha' meant her newly researched thoughts would be erased from his memory by breakfast the next morning.

In their first years of marriage, breakfast was a celebration of waking up in the world together, an intimate ritual before he was called away to the financial front and forced to fight for them both at the office. Now he changed his demeanour like clockwork. Each front door goodbye and driveway departure saw a different man from the one that arrived home. His company car was swallowed up by a motorway of machines that had the same highly addictive nine-to-five needs as him. Financial security was more important than starting a family. That was his firm belief and he stuck to it. Biological warnings passed her by without mention. After all, this was no world to bring a child into, he implied.

Her sense of humanity was still strong this morning, an ability to be concerned about others that somehow would not leave. It was obvious that the time to address her lost years and unfinished business was nearing. The cost of accepting the role of wife was not the issue anymore. A lack of entertainment while waiting for her husband to change his view was now her problem. She could have tried harder to make him change his ways, but naively she swore that she wouldn't be that type of wife. That promise secured his proposal in the first place. She had banked on her husband to align with her wishes eventually. Her gamble didn't play out quite the way she had envisioned. Might it fare better in the end?

Positive action needed to be taken for both their sakes. It was in her own interests as much as his to try and find a solution now. The next few decades would require purpose to her days. He had surpassed his own expectations. He would only retire at the top, sell the company, and live another few years a wealthy man. Unable to admit that money had always been his vice, he claimed each new deal was getting tougher to complete. She had lost him years earlier, when the business started to go international. The past and the reality of the now were beginning to sidetrack her thoughts. Her stride was in need of an incentive. The bookshop was getting near. It would rescue her from herself.

Rows of exotic titles ran the length of the shop, all housed in air-conditioned reverence. Subject matter that very few would explore in their lifetime waited patiently in line for the reader with no preferences. Sometimes inspiration needed a random act of book hunting to create a catalyst for change. She was a firm believer that there was always a book to help her with the matters of her day. History or biographies couldn't compete with satellite TV and a comfortable couch to watch from. Classic fiction? There was no Steinbeck equivalent today. Society has become too comfortable and too willing to remain the victim. Any philosophy from the early 1900s would be diluted too much by media saturation to be deemed fresh and meaningful.

Being of Irish origin herself, it was ironic that the Irish interest section didn't intrigue her. The travel section reminded her that tanning was a solitary activity to be endured in silence, somewhere abroad. Being such a frequent traveller, her husband's lifestyle meant that staying at home on her own was now comfortable for her. Languages had always fascinated her, but the secondary school experience during the 1980s had turned her efforts to learn German into total frustration. Memories of trying to understand the basics required to speak the language without feeling incompetent made her embarrassed to order drinks in Berlin.

Titles recommended by social acquaintances were the books she avoided. Those books were too popular for her, too chat-show friendly and too coffee-table light. She'd listen to their hearsay critique at social functions, but there was little evidence that these people actually read the books. Too much choice was not always a good thing. Her appetite for reading had been flattened by the familiar, expected, and heavily promoted.

An hour had passed, her interests unsatisfied, but the poking about was enjoyable. The bookshop was one of the few places she could be left to decide for herself what to buy. She would purchase some small book out of appreciation for the time and space that the bookshop allowed her. The rest of the day was beginning to look more promising. At some point, she would have to phone himself, give him the all-clear to sleep in the same bedroom again. His leisurely two-and-a-half-hour drive back to Dublin wouldn't phase him. Not in his luxurious car. Driving his pride and joy through the Irish countryside empowered him, allowing him to show the country locals that he was a man of wealth and property now. Wealth had had a negative effect on her marriage so far. Unless he played music they both liked, she usually slept during car trips. It was music that had brought the two of them together as teens, a common appreciation that their parents were unable to take away from them. She reverted to her past sparingly, afraid that the clarity of her fondest memories might fade away too quickly.

Legions of paperback consideration, shelf bound and standing to attention, waiting to be selected and fully explored.

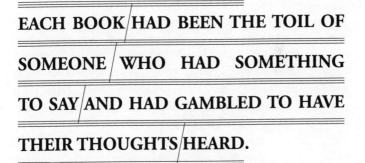

EACH BOOK HAD BEEN THE TOIL OF SOMEONE WHO HAD SOMETHING TO SAY AND HAD GAMBLED TO HAVE THEIR THOUGHTS HEARD.

A bravery she had often admired in the air-conditioned approval of bookshop serenity.

Must move on now.

Leaving the bookshop, Miss turned towards the city centre, its Georgian architecture building up her expectations. Formally rows of residential property, the buildings now housed a variety of businesses. Dublin was great when there was money around. Lately she looked for a sign other than wealth to tell her whether to commit to staying in it. Comparisons to other cities weren't fair. It wasn't London at night or New York in the early spring. She and her husband had visited both cities several times in the nineties. She could have gladly stayed in the Big Apple for much longer. To really enjoy living in Dublin now, she'd need to be twenty-five and single.

The heat of the city pavements had been topped up by a solid week of unseasonable sunshine. Two consecutive days of sunshine could rip up office timetables and turn normally relaxed bars into annoying places for introverts. Extroverts were the main culprits. Cafés and street bars would wrestle an extra table or chair outside to catch one more jaded passer-by. She had seen better café culture abroad, but it was still foreign to many outside the larger cities here. She would not stay long in the city centre today. All the people she knew were in their early forties and hung out in the suburbs, most of them discussing retirement plans or golfing trips that might be added to their business trips abroad.

A seventeen-year-old junkie barrelled out from a small side street, pushing a buggy like he had stolen it. The front wheels were raised high with no child to weigh it down. This stroller was not in the hands of a professional parent. Shopping days told her that real parents tended to take up the middle of the pavement with their prams, at a snail's pace. The youth was probably still tripping from last night's house party. She crossed the street to avoid close contact and pretended not to notice his box of frogs, head movements. Looking for a fix, he used the pram like a lethal weapon to extract money from defenceless pedestrians. He had to decide whether he would blow his cover and cross the street to cut her off. The thought of this teen as a parent disturbed other pedestrians too. They picked up their pace to taxi pass him with elevated chins.

She prayed that the pram wasn't missing a real child as passenger. This is no place to bring a kid up, she thought. If she had her own little one in her mid-twenties, it would be at least seventeen now. Probably tainted by the city and unswayed by her out-of-date wisdom. She had put aside thoughts of being a parent out of loyalty. Her child, if she had one, would have been prepared for a full and productive life by the age of seventeen. She couldn't know for sure, but she half convinced herself that she would never have produced a troubled child, and surely nothing remotely like the seventeen-year-old stroller bandit that she was now trying hard to avoid.

The desperate junkie began to beg aggressively. The buggy was thrown aside. Pockets emptied onto its padded seat while he feverishly separated the copper chaff from the desired wheat of euro coins. The frustration of being short to satisfy a dealer focused his radar. He could still catch that single female who had crossed to the other side. She was too far for his composure to maintain believability, though, and would hear the plastic clatter of a stroller following her at speed. A restaurant door opened, dispensing two girls in their late teens. Miss stepped inside before the door closed and sat down safely at the window seat. The aggravated stroller bandit caught up with the two girls instead.

'Kids. They'll all leave you for their friends at eleven years old,' claimed one of her golfing buddies who had a twenty-nine-year-old 'dud' still living at home. Not everyone would be that unlucky. Teenage souls from her generation had less competition from computer gaming and absolutely none from social media. There was no insurance policy to protect the current batch of children from the perils of the rapid technological evolution. Stroller Bandit struggled hard to remain patient while one of the teenage girls casually fumbled for change in her purse, continuing to chat with her friend. Seated beside the restaurant window, the latest occupant pondered the scene outside in silence 'What elements teamed together to create you, Stroller Bandit?' A terrible sequence of events? The worst kind, no doubt.'

Her husband's decision not to have kids might have been a good call after all. From what she had witnessed today, it could have been so much worse. The waiter didn't interrupt her window gazing. He watched her invest her time watching the junkie religiously kneel before the empty stroller. He commented that the junkie had a quota to reach in order to get high for the day. She decided the menu needed little time to digest; a snap decision for salad and still water would do. By the time her order returned, she had made up her mind on another matter. It was time to text to her husband to say that he could return tomorrow.

The ambient sounds of the city street had no weekday harshness. It lacked the drone of heavy traffic to entertain her in the empty café. The small overpriced salad looked back at her as if to say, Enjoy this time alone; it's not going to last for very long on a day like this. The thought had barely disintegrated when the sledgehammer sound of a head slamming against her window startled her. Stroller Bandit had been knocked with enough force to send him straight back on his rear. Past experience told him to curl up and expect a beating. A female voice interrogated him from out of sight. It sounded like a familiar drill. The voice established the need for a beating once more but not by the Queensbury rules. One hand offered up all his takings. The other shielded his face.

The pavement theatre continued with a sweet female voice of intimidation, the type covering sinister undertones. From stage left, a five-foot-three young woman with a plump two-year-old child draped around her neck came into the spotlight. She appeared to be stronger and less messed up than the creature lying on the ground. Leaning over him to speak without being heard, she kicked him hard enough to say there was more from where that came from. It was obvious to the one-person audience in the café window that Stroller Bandit was not long for this world. Having to accept that amount of abuse from a pint-sized tyrant would ensure it. As for the child, he had dismissed all authority long ago, with the exception of his mother.

The fighting couple failed to acknowledge the Garda patrol car sail up with its passenger window down. Ringside seats for its two female occupants. Their engine idled before they parked several feet from the scene, waiting to see if the situation warranted intervention or a cup of coffee. The waiter went to the doorway and made himself known to both officers with hand signals. He also alerted the stomach-kicking tyrant to the police presence parked behind her. Law and Order were forced to make a move now that they had been exposed. The Tyrant sensed their approach and transformed into victim mode without any noticeable effort.

The café's sole customer was impressed by the attacker's agile strategy. She tried to predict the sequence of events. First, Tyrant starts the tear ducts on demand. Second, Tyrant presents the child to the two officers. Third, Tyrant blames the irresponsibility of the Stroller Bandit for causing all the trouble because he's already known to the authorities. Fourth, Tyrant points to the collapsed stroller before crying into the stupefied face of her child.

She thought that she had predicted accurately from the safety of her café seat, but, to her surprise, the Tyrant was placed in the back of the patrol car with her child, while the other officer immediately went to give assistance to the clearly distressed Stroller Bandit still on the ground. Things were beginning to take a serious turn for Stroller Bandit, and it looked like an ambulance would be required. Another patrol car passed on the other side of the street and quickly made a U-turn to offer assistance. The waiter got the distinct feeling that both he and his only customer in the café would be questioned. With one foot either side of the threshold, he leaned back and looked his customer in the eye, implying she had seen more than he had. He was washing his hands clean. She froze in her seat at the possibility of being a witness. All she could imagine was her husband's voice remarking, 'I leave you alone for one day.' She would respond if the police needed to talk to her. The officer attending Stroller Bandit ceased his ministrations on hearing the ambulance siren echo off the Georgian building facades.

The other officer walked briskly through the door, her notebook already at work. Her calm voice suggested she was a professional consultant. After details were taken, she asked her interviewee if she had any questions. Her interviewee just asked if Mr. Stroller Bandit was badly hurt. The officer politely revealed that the victim may have had his pride and manhood realigned. A fractured or broken rib was the initial guess, but that could have happened earlier. Both women exchanged contact details in case there were further developments, but he wouldn't press any charges. He never did because of the child. The officer thanked her for her help; she was free to go. Notebook folded, her duty done. The waiter told his only customer to stay as long as she wanted, offering her a new seat away from the window.

Catching her reflection in the wall mirror advertisement for some French liqueur, she found an unexpected alliance, and she discreetly asked her reflection if she had done the right thing by getting out of bed that morning. Being safely tucked away from the taunts of the city all week was convenient, to a point. She didn't deny that her lifestyle could distract her from everyday street concerns. Anything that might prove unpleasant to her but sensational to the masses could be ignored with the help of her domestic duties. Coffee mornings and club meetings were there to shelter her from witnessing reality.

Her mobile phone produced a giddy, animated chime on the table as the waiter dropped a complimentary cappuccino in front of her. It was her husband returning her text message. It was obvious even to the waiter that, while her wedding band spoke of a marriage, her vacant stare suggested one party might be going through the motions. Her marital contract needed updates in its small print before it was renewed. She was about to return the text but decided to phone him instead; he deserved that at least. How about if she took a train down there and stayed for a week, and they could sort this out? The voice on the other end went into overdrive. She had made someone's day, the waiter observed.

6

BEDROCK

| | | | | | |?|-|"" |0|

,

The location of Morty's bar on Main Street left no space outside for staff to smoke a cigarette with any degree of privacy. No nooks or architectural crannies to help conceal their tobacco addiction. There was no point in employees trying to hide the fact that (A) they were not working to their true potential and (B) there never were any customers inside the bar this early on a Sunday. Customers that did happen to pass by would frequently ask the smoking sentry if there was anyone inside. A simple but wise question to avoid being ambushed by the Sub or someone else they'd like to avoid completely. Today's advice to passers-by was that it might be in their interests to continue on with their Sunday walk.

Alone inside the empty bar sat a silent car wreck wearing expensive pinstripes, slumped on fixed forearms with a suspended stare competing with his spotless reflection in the mirror behind the counter. Face-off negotiations with himself were out of character. He was known for his work ethic and shrewd business deals over the last fifteen years, but he was not known for daytime drinking. Something must have happened or been accepted recently. He was obsessed with business, and all his promises to cut back on the unholy hours were easily forgotten until he had reached this point. She had left him briefly once before, out of frustration. It had happened while he went to Glasgow, securing another chance for profit, another crowning piece in his expanding empire. There was reason for her departure other than that he was not there for her. No other man in her life, no kids, no joy, no nothing. He could have his work all to himself since it was truly the only relationship he was consumed with. Gifts, foreign holidays, unsubtle sweeteners for future business breaks were all rejected. His potential business success was a major factor in attaining her parents' blessing for their engagement and marriage eighteen years ago. They wanted her to be happy and secure. He'd never realised his desire for financial advancement would eventually push her aside. It didn't take too many years before she started to join various health clubs and societies, all out of basic neglect.

The car wreck at the counter heaved slowly through pints of stout and shots of reminiscence. He couldn't blame her for threatening to pack her bags. All marriages have to go through peaks and troughs. The troughs in this case had considerably outnumbered the peaks, though. She had endured waiting for him for too long. To outsiders he appeared hurt by the situation; it was disappointment. He could have tried harder to make it work, but he just didn't make the effort in the same way he strived to make his business work. Business was a language he knew. It protected him from failure and gave him authority to manipulate his fate, or so he thought. Today he drank and thought of his wedding anniversary.

The irony was that it was the first time in years he didn't have to be reminded by her. He accepted his negligence and hoped she'd let him patch things up in any way he could. Everyone in Dublin believed that they both were better off separated. Attitudes had changed from the old days of watching American soap stars divorcing ten times over, the house and kids split down the middle. Failure was usually failure in the eyes of others. Was he cheating? Was the business in trouble? Was he having a meltdown? The business that he built up, the same one that had consumed his marriage, was finally turning on him, and not in a playful way.

It had taken too long to admit that he had seen the signs of her retreat into the shade of his success. There was no excuse. No number of achieved monthly targets could justify allowing his stay-at-home wife to hold herself hostage. He had manipulated the concept of marriage as an excuse to enable her to do so. This town wouldn't take long to make up its mind on the issue of whether the marriage was destined to survive or not. Marriages should last longer than businesses. His wealth impressed very few here. There were too few opportunities for it to shine. Wealthy people only came home to visit at Christmas and left in the New Year. High finance was the domain of the city, and local concerns did not make front-page news of The Financial Times. The Forbes 500 could be an expensive brand of artificial fertilizer around here.

The absence of other drinkers reassured the solitary customer seated at the bar counter that wallowing was allowed today. Sundays were brutally slow, right up until eight o'clock at night. The stiffness had vacated his suit. It could have been a wet blanket for all the presence it gave him. His car keys dared him to get caught, way over the limit, banned from working. Might be easier to be imprisoned for a year and get sorted. Tabula rasa, start from scratch, learn from the whole mess, and make amends. Time to cut ties with the city and prevent getting tangled up in its noose. Outside, the barman smoked, knowing there was no danger of theft at half two in the afternoon.

The front door had jammed and was shoulder-shoved open, startling the low-lit room with a fresh blast of light. Old hinges strained heavily as the door closed slowly behind the barman's stride. His active pace suggested there would be no conference calls with him today. He had intent etched all over his face and moved about like he had just been informed that his judgmental relatives were coming to visit. Dust the bar with purpose. Give a weekly wipe to the shelves. The barman's activity contrasted sharply with the stillness of the only customer present. Years earlier this customer might have looked or acted with the same feverish diligence. Now he felt there was more to life than work disguised as the pursuit of happiness.

Another weekend visit to the home town. It was all that his business duties would allow these days. A show of face and parade of success for the last time before his private life became a public nudge, wink, and smirk. Maybe it was a token gesture of regret for discarding his roots and only turning up when the fan couldn't take any more crap. Or maybe it was a long held belief that blood is thicker than water. An unspoken belief that he hoped to have confirmed. He would be explaining himself to his father without fear, if it wasn't too late, as the man who allowed him to shape himself as an individual with little interference. His father might have to revise his definition of the word 'proud', as it used to pertain to his eldest son. He would call Ninja later and see if he'd finished the Meals on Wheels run.

The stone-faced man politely propped up at the counter invited the barman to analyse his demeanour silently. All signs pointed to a death in his life. The heaviness of the fixed stare meant the loss of something important to him alone. Gut reaction said that it had to be more family than friend. The man's facial expression was too serious for weather talk and too quiet for sports talk. He seemed the type that couldn't talk politics without raising his voice. His 'don't bother me today' body language thundered. The barman guessed that the visitor was used to analysing others rather than allowing himself to be analysed. It made him wonder if customers ever tried to read their own poker face. Suddenly he stood stationary, his long-term memory bubbling, bringing a familiar face to the surface. He broke the silence of the bar. 'Ninja,' the barman blurted with relief. 'The brother?'

A small nod and slow smile signalled his willingness to order another pint, but his 'no conversation please' eyes meant the barman's probe would have to be left as a single jab at striking up conversation. Just like in the boardroom meetings. Stillness must be controlled before any momentous acts of bravery were considered. No need to fortify reluctance with alcohol. He would never dare meet his father in a heap. It would be better to speak directly to Ninja first. His big city mind was made up. Shoulders lightened, conscience dusted, and purpose fixed. His father would not be disappointed for very long. The old man always moved onward when situations had already taken their course. He had a policy when it came to dealing with difficulties that presented themselves in life and encouraged both sons not to pick at things when they were broken. The man should have studied philosophy, maybe psychology of some form. No family obstacle seemed to faze him, but, more important, the old man never once said 'I told you so', not to Ninja or himself, in words or demeanour. Maybe his silence was worse. Maybe he should say something today and clear the air. This time, his father might reveal a flaw in his armour or a lack of tolerance for his favourite son.

The barman's ears didn't prick up on seeing his only customer look at his phone. It looked like he was deciding to make an unpleasant phone call. He didn't want to appear like he was eavesdropping or hungry for insider gossip. A perfect excuse to fill a bucket with hot soapy water, wring a rag, and march out the front door. Pub privacy for phone calls was not expected, and opportune moments were a lottery. Ninja's brother rarely rang him unless to check if their father was in good form. Later the barman would ring the old man. If his father was not himself, he'd ring with big news, good news. If his father was in good form, he'd listen to him chat. But the frequency of that was getting less and less. The old man wasn't well.

　　The brother scrolled down his illuminated handset and debated whether to phone his father or Ninja. The phone rang out only twice before Ninja responded. The loud background interference of Ninja's van at speed greeted his older brother's ear. The bad coverage made Ninja's end of the line sound more like some WWII bomber pilot flying through heavy flak. Unfamiliar shrieks alerted him to the fact that his brother was not alone, but he enquired anyway. It seemed there were two Americans along for the ride for some Emerald Isle postcard opportunities. The two novice members of Ninjas Sunday air crew whooped and screamed. The intermittent breaks in transmission made it difficult to decipher Ninja's replies completely. Not a good time to make this call. A suds-smack of a wet rag on the pub window claimed ownership of the bar silence but from the outside. Figure eights in white bubbled streaks skated across the main pub window. Ninja's brother felt like he was trapped inside of a washing machine before the rinse cycle commenced. The dolphin noises of a window squeegee clearing pristine paths prised a smile from the sole sipper. Each swipe illuminated the inside of the bar with the faint light that the outside world offered. The barman was doing a sterling job, and his window-cleaning bore no signs of being a chore. The brother grabbed his phone once more and furiously texted a message to meet up with Ninja later.

start scan

As soon as a wet sponge touches a window pane
you must commit. Balancing on a low stool
outside the goldfish bowl of delegated
authority, the barman could easily
lose his composure to the taunts
from marauding teenagers.

perimeter check

{ PAUSE }

interior check

A small light disturbed the   A solitary text-faced glow
interior darkness.   was nothing for him
                              to be concerned
                              about today.

,

scan complete

Porpoise sounds of window-cleaning were too energetic for the man sitting in stillness. He needed to think but hadn't the determination to focus. The decision to hoist himself off the bar stool coincided with the return of the cleaning bucket to its place of privilege beneath the bar counter. The last residue of stout disappeared during the act of straightening himself up. His reaction time rattled his ability to put his trench coat back on. He should brief Ninja first before throwing the bad news before his father. Consideration was the least he could offer his brother.

The therapeutic low light of the bar did not prepare him for a daytime exit or the sight of his brother's face plastered on a poster outside. Ninja seemed oddly comfortable in the protective shadow of two guys in balaclavas. It amazed him to see public proof of this part of his brother's personality. The poster made him wonder if his younger brother was in the proper state of mind to understand the gravity of his current marriage problems. He appeared to project the right attitude to life, though. Don't take the majority of it so seriously. If both brothers were struck dead by a bolt of lightning, which of them would have achieved more satisfaction in life? All the eldest had achieved was an above-average standard of living amongst the Dublin elite. Somewhere in there, he might have lost a wife too.

Another poster appeared on a telegraph pole, an older gig date with two bronzed, black-bikini-wearing females in balaclavas. Ninja appeared in the same pose as in the previous poster. Both posters had something else in common. There was no visible trace of photographic manipulation. It was a professional studio shot, perfectly lit, the typography well considered to emphasise Ninja's cold, farcical 'Holly-wouldn't take me seriously' face. All cleverly staged to communicate to the public that he had invested in his act and it was worth a look, if not a laugh. Ninja always had a natural ability to understand how to get ordinary people's attention. Bigger entertainers might get the same effect, but he didn't go for the cheap option, and it showed. What he lacked in performance, he made up for in production.

The hotel was clean and looked after, refurbished during the good times. Having had the privilege of staying in five-star hotels all over the world usually brought up comparisons. Not today. The clerk assured him his car was perfectly safe. Descriptions of all of the services available to him evaded his attention, but he waited without interrupting her. She drew a last breath to finish the rehearsed safety procedures and breakfast time information, and finally pointed to the elevator. The clerk failed to mention that this hotel had to be a contender for operating the world's smallest elevator.

Hotel room clichés continued to wander around his mind as he unpacked. They reminded him momentarily of important deals before the reason for this weekend trip reminded him of his personal vulnerability. Deal with it. Get the situation addressed and resolved quickly. He couldn't look in the wall mirror without imagining the ladies in the last poster and wondering if he would be able to parade himself like Ninja. Not in corporate Dublin, he wouldn't. Not him. Power-dressing was a strength. Presentation was a seducer and also an informer. Before any charcoal word fell from his mouth, let them know how much of a big shot they were dealing with. All well and good, but what about when he was out of his comfort zone?

A power nap on the king-sized bed and a shower straight after was required. That would knock the fatigue clear out of sight and prepare him for an audience with Ninja. That feeling of being unable to match the strength and determination of his earlier years was beginning to creep in. Keep up the appearance of being in control, focused, and decisive. Never appear too preoccupied or distracted infront of those you need most. Weight was difficult to keep down, especially at the age of fifty-five. A fat-cat body shape is not a good look for newspaper photographs. Be swift, exact, and unforgiving. Looking intelligent is one thing; falling for that look could be financially disastrous. There were boardrooms all around the capital brimming with eager young business executives who would fall hard for that look every single time. Yes-men would always be the easiest targets for that look.

He had twenty minutes to nap before he blindly swept the alarm clock for its elusive snooze button. Wake up. Don't dwell too much on it; just act. A routine drill. The shower would forgive you for every previous day. Exposed, with no pinstriped armour to hide behind. The business suit did much of the initial talking for you when you were afraid to admit that you were wrong. With all of his material wealth and trappings of success, it had boiled down to one personal creature comfort. The one thing that could not be intruded upon was taking a shower. Only when the relaxing effects of the shower were achieved was it time to move. The mocking mirror demanded that he shave carefully before he left.

Being part of the big city circus act lost more of its allure. Now every day forced him to go through the motions like everyone else. Casual clothes could not be worn comfortably any more. He had dressed in boardroom battledress for too long, parading along delegated ramparts far from danger. Too smart for trouble, but too stupid to remember his own house was not immune to grief. He had to respect his wife for her endurance. She would be the one to come out smelling of roses financially if the marriage failed. That could enhance her chances at another relationship. Not the time to call her now. His second sweater selection was rejected by the mirror in favour of a black polo neck. His brass neck would be less evident. His double chin dared to show its presence.

Was it all for nothing? Eighteen years of graft, of forking out for a five-bedroom house in south Dublin and his wife alone in it. It must have been worse for her. A glorified lighthouse for all the company she had. The office, the numerous airport meetings, the vulgar limousines, the hotel rooms, and those annoying discussions in business bars instead of spending time at home with her. He had valid reasons to be away, at least on paper. Not good enough, not one bit fair. She had told him that countless times before. Now thick silence greeted him from the living room each night. When had all this become obvious to her? She had been consumed by his business long before he had.

The reflective elevator walls showed him the back of his head. Was this what she saw as he left for the office each day? It was inevitable that a successful streak of fifteen years would reveal a kink somewhere along the line. Complacency … a bad choice of word for greed. He'd have to hold his hand up high, mea culpa. The fault was his alone, not hers. His worst assumption was that she'd hang in there while he concentrated on the needs of the office. It was time to minimise his workload if she was to stay.

The elevator reached the ground floor and opened its narrow doors to the ambient tones of hoovering from the floor above. A good hotel is always a busy hotel. The clerk could clearly tell that he did not need assistance. She kept her trained smile of availability fixed, tracking him as he walked by. Task completed, she returned to her phone queries, confident of his passing. Lounge bound, an empty bay window beckoned him to sit and wait beside it. If there were tourists in the vicinity, he would avoid them. This was not a hotel for mingling with its mixed bag of guests. Experience projected a lack of tolerance for soft chat, especially at the mention of weather. Discussions about the weather were only tolerated when it threatened to prevent him from playing a game of golf.

He had no desire to drink more alcohol. A cup of coffee and newspaper would relax him. Thankfully his predictable brother was never known to be intentionally late, a family trait instilled throughout their childhood. It was extremely disrespectful to keep anyone waiting. Being sent to the butcher and not remembering what you were supposed to ask for was shameful; it made your family look foolish and absent-minded. Don't expect other people to run on your time, his father would tell him. You need to be aware of other people's time and they'll remember your consideration. Simple instructions like these had helped both brothers to attain the reliability tag from community leaders. They were trusted to heed the changing agenda of the small town. The result was offhand advice from town elders, respected figures who had provided his family with extra crumbs of wisdom.

He'd wait for Ninja. The front bay-window seat of the hotel lounge would make it easier to witness his brother's dramatic entrance in panoramic comfort. Being the elder sibling, the assumption was that he was the logical, more seasoned son. It suited him to think so. She had left him before. For a split second he wondered if he had the patience for anyone else any longer. He was wealthy enough to say goodbye to this country. His father had heard worse, just not from him. Breaking the uncertain news was a precautionary route to take and one that might prevent his father having a heart attack later on. He would have to be patient and hear Ninja's assessment of his father's health first. Tonight, may not be the best time to inform his younger sibling of his marital disharmony.

Waiting for his brother to make an appearance was taxing his composure. He was not comfortable now that the effects of the shower had worn off. The house newspaper shielded him from displaying any hint of restlessness, an admission of anxiety, but his family knew him better. That was the benefit when sharing with family; most knew how to understand and not judge each other too quickly. They had known him long before he had acquired his Dublin 4 briefcase. Ninja could dismantle his older brother quickly, brick by painful brick. His father … he could raze him to the ground with ease. Neither of them were to be lied to.

The bay-window view had nothing new to tell him. All the new buildings stood near the edge of town and away from main street eyes. He could remember his youth when the town belonged to all. Back then small towns raised everyone's kids. Parents worked hard and flung their kids into the arms of its streets, teasing them to play until dark. Ninja was always sent to fetch him from friends in neighbouring streets. Shouting that their Dad wanted them both home in the next five minutes, or else, worked every time. In those days 'or else' had consequences with bruises attached. It was their father's way of extracting his eldest son from older peers that got to stay out later and get into trouble sooner. He only intervened to protect the integrity of his sons. Ninja's van finally crept into view.

CHAPTER

7

GLITCH

| | | | | | | | |-|""|0|

?

Their father's bedroom was sacred. As long as his authority ruled their household, neither son dared to cross its threshold. They had been brought up in a happy house which had unspoken rules. Everyone had his or her own territory and privacy. It was a big house with bedrooms for all and more for guests that no longer visited. The kitchen had been their mother's domain, and nobody entered unannounced. It had grown quiet without her presence.

A noticeable shift in weighted footsteps upstairs alerted the sitting-room vigil that the medical examination had concluded. Cautious stairway steps staggered the retiring doctor's descent, commanding both brothers to stand to attention. They remembered the doctor's last visit. It had signalled a profound transfer of power within their household. Their kitchen doorway manners demanded by their mother had lost all their integrity through her illness. Her domain became just another room in the house, but with fewer rules. They remembered how the doctor's prognosis for her had rapidly changed from hope to resignation.

Ninja listened intently to the medical appraisal while his brother scanned the doctor for tells. The medicine man gave nothing away. Blood tests and scans had confirmed Alzheimer's. He paraded symptoms along a hierarchy of fingers to emphasize his diagnosis. The elder brother continued to vet the doctor's delivery.

Second opinions annoyed the businessman used to life on the clock. He usually required concise information from his staff and no second guesses. Ninja needed to believe that there might be hope in the delayed confirmation. Regardless, they agreed that their father's mental state was no longer the rock that they had revered all their lives. Who would this man be then?

The doctor left the house with professional respect for his long-time valued acquaintance. Small town doctors and their intimate circle of close friends always had to keep a certain distance under the guise of professionalism. Illness was a social disease in a small town, and it wasn't wise to make weak deals with rural doctors. You did exactly as they demanded.

The question of what to do now hung heavy over their parents' house. One parent had left the earth physically; the other might not return spiritually. Both brothers began to consider their own lifespans. Upstairs the lightly sedated old man that they called their father lay in bed. His title was drifting away from its paternal meaning. They had no experience in comforting each other, and the moment vaporised with the willingness to venture upstairs to the elderly man's bedside. To watch the last remnants of his memory slip into fantasy. The realisation that the guardian of their world was about to lose his context in it did not sit well with either son. Others might suggest that they too could suffer the same fate years down the road.

Ninja wondered if he would spend his life breaking his back, only to be found by neighbours, gazing through some garden window, oblivious to all around him. Surely their father had more to say, but they'd never know how much was withheld from them now. His experience could no longer be called upon to untangle their moral knots or contemporary reasoning. From now on, all of their father's worldly advice would have its origins questioned. Indecisive shrugs from one sibling to the other cancelled authority. Nevertheless, Ninja had no intention of being the first one to break the house rule. His braver brother was not so keen either, but necessity overrode his fear. Neither brother needed a needle to drop to establish their father's sedated state upstairs. The deep bass snoring was clearly audible from behind the privacy of the bedroom door.

Ninja led his brother to their father's bedroom door before turning slowly around and suggesting that seniority should venture first. Cringing at the door handle, prepared for some unwelcome surprise, the elder gently knocked for forgiveness before entering. Darkness draped the peaceful body asleep under a raised quilted mass. Eyes adjusted to the low light as the two stepped in unison towards their father's bed. The eldest had an uncomfortable thought. Somewhere in the recesses of his father's mind, his number one son might have been misplaced, taken to a world that he could never access again.

Ninja surveyed the bedroom in awe, quietly sloping towards the framed secrets of its walls. There were definitely stories locked inside this room. Each photograph captured a single moment in the evolution of their father's personality with expressions he could recognise in his brother and himself but at odds with the living colour version asleep in front of them. The wall was full of candid moments from the past: of embarrassment with the girl that would later become his wife, that county final, graduation night, saving hay with neighbours, at some local dance, standing in the distance behind Mother, his wedding day, his proud wife, their mother. The bedroom wall timeline of photographs came to an abrupt end before his two sons were born. What life lesson was so awful as to declare this room off limits all their lives? What did he feel so strongly about that warranted such protection? Had their father tried to hang onto happier times now that she had gone? Stationary in the stillness of the old man's breath, his sons felt less important in his presence. There was no longer any time in this life to impress him.

The brothers turned away from the sepia memories of a life more interesting than their own, leaving them to watch over the secret life of the great man. Ninja's imagination was compelled to project the facial expressions from the photographs onto his father's sleeping mask in a bid to see which ones fixed. He was a different man from the one they eagerly grew up for, this mystery man who applied himself to whatever needs gravitated his way in life. There was duty to others regardless of the situation; it was his brand of humanity.

A deep, slow breathing pattern rhythmically churned its way around the bedroom. In the mature aroma of their father's sanctuary, both brothers became nervous. They readied to leave in soft, measured strides, but they heard the sound of unconscious ramblings, stopping them statue-still again. Mumbled words broke free from their father's mouth in several broken contexts but seemed to be struggling to attach themselves to some imaginary conversation. The brothers strained to decipher some fragments of meaning from his gibberish. What secrets was he be wrestling with?

TENSE |THE PRESENT | **CONFUSED**

THE PAST | REFUSED | # TENSE

TENSE |THE FUTURE | **BEMUSED**

TWO STEPS BACK & ONE

———————→ ALL TAKE AND NO GIVING BACK

STEP FORWARD, ALL THIS

———————→ BUT YOU STILL CRY FOR MORE

WILL BE YOURS SOMEDAY,

———————→ AS IF IT'S THE VERY FIRST TIME

MY TWO SONS & ~~DAUGHTER.~~

———————→ YOU HAVE. SAME BLOODY STORY.

Ðⓒñ™ INDUS.COM

PROTECTED YOU FOR YEARS, NOT AN OUNCE OF THANKS.

WHO PAVED THE WAY THROUGH LIFE FOR BOTH OF YOU?

Married with kids at the age of twenty-five, investing all that time for fifty years, just

to see them from the inside of a nursing home? I bet you think you're pretty smart.

Think you can survive on your own? You'll have to help each pother without me soon.

WILL	YOU	EVER	KNOW	WHO	YOU	REALLY	ARE?
SURE,	YOU'LL	BOTH	MAKE	DO,	YOU	ALWAYS	DID.

The eldest brother didn't take to his father's unconscious stream of thought too comfortably. Ninja sensed that this nervousness was a signal for both of them to withdraw. The two looked back once more at the whispering heap, knowing that it was unlikely there would be a recovery. Their old man was someone else. What lay behind could have been a stranger that needed a roof for the night. Tragedies had always seemed to happen to other people before this. Neither of them spoke about it out loud, but it looked like their father was going to need professional care. A kick to both their egos. The justification wouldn't require much discussion. All conversation from this point would be with this man as opposed to the person they had known before. Friends that hadn't shared their feelings with him before would feel hard done by now. Tragedies could be unexpectedly cruel that way. It was too late for both sons now. Their words would have to be powerful indeed to register with this version of their father.

The bedroom wall of photographs suggested that the old man had left both his sons no wiser to his inner workings or to the person he truly was. A private man with a warm public persona, rarely witnessed by his sons. Layer after deflected public layer preserved an intimacy that had been shared only with his wife long before her own battle with illness had ended. Now they envied her time with him.

The brothers would have to start from scratch. Whether they liked it or not, they had to live with the memories they knew to be true. Prior to this, they had only memories they believed to be true. They had to trust the doctor's opinion. The doctor probably knew more about their father than either son did. There seemed to be an unwritten law that the passing generation should reveal little of their wisdom or secret beliefs to the next crop.

In a slow, purposeful descent downstairs with synchronised steps, both brothers headed intuitively for the heart of the house. The electric kettle was inspected for water before being slung underneath the cold tap, ready to be filled. Creating acoustic tension in the kitchen, it reverted to a grumble after reaching the boiling point.

Propped up against the kitchen sink, Ninja folded his arms to refrain from biting his nails. He felt slightly ashamed for thoughts of betrayal by the bedroom wall. So many photographs but none of him. His brother sat at the kitchen table and proceeded to stare intensely at a spot on the floor. 'Take it easy, Ninja ... Dad is by no means dead yet. No matter what the doctor comes back with, he's not gone yet, alright?' He delivered short, considered sentences whenever he was in danger of revealing his emotions. They were going to have to start acting on this soon, and that was for sure. Time to start coming up with a few realistic options.

Ninja took a deep breath with his back facing his brother. He conceded that his brother's business mind might be appropriate in this situation. No time for emotion. Their father's future needed proper planning. Ninja admitted that he knew no alternative to placing their father in care if the doctor recommended it. If not, he would have to bear the responsibility of taking care of his father's health because he was the only one living at home.

His brother broke from his stare and stood up from the table to a full boardroom press, head bowed. 'You'd really do that too?' he asked and thought some more. They needed to carry out this duty, their duty, without reservation. Both brothers felt slightly alien to the bricks and mortar they had commonly referred to as their home. A home for Ninja at least. The elder brother began to consider himself homeless. His trophy Dublin castle had become no more than an expensive hostel lately. Their family house was fully owned and had been proudly paid for by their father's hard work. The site had been handed down by their mother. Legal paperwork decreed it would be shared between the brothers equally unless the will had changed in the last few years. Ninja deserved the house; it seemed right according to the brother. All those years in the shade, struggling to survive. They would wait for the doctor to report back, hoping for something less traumatic than Alzheimer's. The eldest was making a list of all possible consequences in his head. As things stood, his father wouldn't have to hear of his marriage problems now.

Neither son could be totally sure of their old man's medical history. Making contact with distant relatives who lived in nearby towns was probably a good move. The more approachable ones might be able to fill in some of the medical blanks concerning their family tree, providing insight to their father's condition. Ninja didn't want to hear too much of this. It could mean that all the memories of their hard-earned achievements and experience of the past might be wiped clean in the near future. The elder brother cared less about his personal identity; it had been confirmed by business and financial success. Ninja gained his identity by living in a community that changed reluctantly over time. There would be some locals who wouldn't care if either brother inherited their fathers condition.

None of their mother's nearest relatives had bothered to step through the front door of their rural house in more than fifteen years. Their father's neither. Ninja always thought that the Celtic Tiger economic fallout provided more pressing engagements than extended family get-togethers with them. Invitations to weddings (that they were not expected to attend) and thinly disguised requests to his brother for Munster rugby tickets in Thomond Park were the only reason some of these people ventured to visit. His brother's success in the city helped to keep their snobbery at bay. It created a welcome diversion when conversation ventured into ridiculing Ninja's antics. They considered Ninja the least ambitious family member because of his life choices. His brother's wealth helped them to keep those cheap assumptions to themselves.

Sunday evening at eight o'clock was usually when the elder son phoned his father from Dublin, and, until recently, he scarcely failed. He chose to call at a time when Ninja was at work. It was convenient to update the old man then and share his plans for the week. His father could make tenuous connections into strong ones, even from outside his son's business domain, by providing information that could help change the outcome of a golf course chat. The climax of each Sunday call was awkwardly reserved for questions based on how the other was doing. But not today.

Ninja made himself scarce when the phone rang on Sunday nights. Whether it was his brother or work, unexpected phone calls could spoil plans. His father spoke more freely to his elder brother on those Sunday phone calls than to Ninja all week. As long as one of his sons was successful … well, that was the impression his father gave but without saying it directly to his face. At this very moment, both offspring were equally useless. The logical brother stared at the ceiling intently, cogs turning, pros and cons settling into different categories of yeses, noes, maybes. Ninja assumed that all his brother's decisions would be based on what was best for his father's situation.

Bother could make it appear to his business associates that his father's illness had something to do with the breakup of his marriage. An unwritten rule of success was that someone close would eventually affect your business edge. Keep it real tight at home, or at least appear to be happy and content on the outside. A break from work for family reasons sounded pretty vague and open to abuse. Returning home to take care of your father was an impressive reason amongst businessmen. Many got their initial financial stake from their fathers and their fathers before them. His unhappy wife would help out; she could also use it as an excuse for their marital problems. Ninja noticed his brother's contemplative look and glanced at his mobile phone until the other snapped out of his thoughts.

Who knew exactly what that bedroom wall meant to the man asleep upstairs? Today they had realised that they had not paid the same attention to their father in the last few years. The distance between all three had expanded unnoticed. Who could Ninja trust to show the photos to with complete confidentiality? Couldn't be anyone too close to the family. Not the doctor but maybe Bart? With Bart, there might be inaccuracies where dates were concerned but not with faces. Last Thursday might be completely lost, but not fifty years ago or more. He could probably recognise everyone in the old photos. It had been ages since Ninja sat in silence with anyone other than his father and he felt the need to delete Bother from his contact list and replace it with The Brother.

Ninja brought the digital camera in from the van and upstairs to his father's bedroom. The rise and fall his father's breathing coincided with Ninja's compositional checks. Each photograph on his father's wall of fame was carefully documented. Turning to leave the wheezing-filled room, he paused with bowed head and took his father's portrait while there was still blood flowing through those veins. He tentatively fixed the bedcovers before retaking the shot, both portrait and landscape. Too late to capture the man's spirit. The drugs had allowed deep sleep to wash over. No need to tell anyone that he had taken advantage of the moment. It might be something he could show the brother another time.

Ninja printed the shots out on high-gloss printer paper. All those faces looking back, reborn in their second life as printouts. Bart would have little difficulty analysing the faces, his eyes still razor sharp and trained to hunt nostalgia. His brother assessed the quality with a sequence of approving nods. They couldn't leave their father alone from now on, which meant only one could be present when Bart unravelled the secrets housed in the images from the past. Clearly Ninja had to get Bart to talk. He would have to be trusted to gauge the accuracy of Bart's memory because his brother would not be able to observe the interview from home. It would be impossible to sift through Bart's body language and verbal delivery from there. Being in control was his brother's main source of energy.

The thought of getting some context or confirmation to the photographs from an outside source rather than from their extended family was comforting. Family secrets could be more shocking if uncovered by the wrong relatives. Being prepared was essential. Ninja pointed the camera at Bother to break the tension. His brother barely produced a smile. This plan with Bart was obviously more important to him than to Ninja. He knew there was definite potential here to distract others from his marital problems in Dublin. He would require just the right amount of sympathy to maintain integrity when he returned to the big city interrogations. His personal life would only be resolved with an honest strategy.

?

NOW WAS THE TIME TO CONSIDER
LIFE WITHOUT THE OLD MAN.
IT WOULD BE POINTLESS
TO DO SO BEFOREHAND.

With only a fridge

to hold sentry

[IT GOT REAL QUIET]

THE HEART OF THE HOUSE WAS LOSING ITS WARMTH

acceptance could only

be digested

in silence

The sound of the fridge discreetly interrupted their kitchen contemplation with a perfectly timed cooling cycle. It made Ninja think of nights he'd returned home from the bar late and sat in the cold kitchen silence on his own. 'Y'know, it's a damn pity that you didn't convince Miss to take the trip down this weekend. Could've been handy. We could both talk to Bart then.'

His brother switched focus on hearing these words and returned to his seat to stare once more at the floor. It was highly likely that Miss would be mentioned at some stage by Ninja, the two of them had always been kindred spirits. Bother knew if Ninja had asked his wife, she'd have left her comfortable living room couch in Dublin for their father, especially if she knew the difficulty they were in. The old man loved her presence and energy as it sailed from room to room. He'd warned his son that she wasn't to be left behind as his business hours started to eat into their time together. She was always a source of motivation behind the scenes until his business began to soar. He knew that second fiddle was not a position she naturally accepted. Unfortunately, second fiddle was exactly what she had become these days. Ninja placed two cups on the kitchen counter with enough force to snap his brother out of another contemplative state. Careful planning was still needed, and he would drink as much tea as it took until it was sorted. Ninja asked his brother about herself and if she was keeping well. Uncomfortable shoulder shifts by the elder signalled that an unexpected answer may be on its way. Ninja stirred his tea with slow purpose and prepared himself to listen.

'We're going through a rough patch. She was thinking of leaving again, tired of being on her own. Don't blame her. Before you start jumping to any conclusions, there is nobody else involved,' he said. Ninja supped his tea slowly. A deep breath suggested that his brother didn't want to discuss it anymore but was relieved that he had said his piece. He hoped Ninja would understand. Ninja stood up from his seat and pretended to be unconcerned by the fridge's decision to revert to silence.

CHAPTER

8

INNOCENT

There's a certain noise that a tea cup can make in anger, regardless of whose kitchen you may be sleeping above. Then there is the sound of a second cup receiving a thorough lecture from a tea towel before being scolded onto the sideboard. As if that weren't its first warning, another sharp ceramic smack on the fake marbled worktop is the clincher. You're out of this woman's life the moment you open your lying mouth. There would be nobody to blame but yourself. No blank expression on your face will absolve you. She'll slam that big front door in a minute. Its frame will shed splinters from rage. Don't you dare be caught lounging around her house when she gets home.

The front door slammed violently. That was the sound of two (and a bit) years walking away. Mind made up, she cradled her handbag like some defensive child unexpectedly called out for lying. This was not her usual clutch-grip confidence. Her pavement pace challenged the structural soundness of her shoe heels. His first thoughts were of how much this argument would cost him. Dole day today. Rent due, food, and cigarettes for the next seven days would dictate how much money was available to patch up the relationship. Today did not feel like a day for fighting with her or, in his case, getting whipped. A distraction of sorts would be welcome, something with a surprising get-out-of-jail feel to it. Now his thoughts would be free from interruption. Stretching his body muscles to their fullest, bed aerobics made his feet stick out from under the duvet and hang over the end of the bed. She must have spotted something to place all door hinges on high alert. She was capable of winding herself up at a moment's notice but these eruptions usually took place when he was within striking distance. The weight of the nearest projectile had to be factored into account too. What did she find? What made her flip from being content to irate? A broad yawn and a clutch of dominance with her scented pillow were interrupted by a thought, the type that could unravel most people. Could she have overheard something about him? Hardly. She seemed just fine last night. What could she have dug up between then and this morning?

He couldn't sleep in now. There must be some clue to that dramatic exit. Some evidence downstairs in the kitchen would provide the most believable defence to employ later. He had gone through this before. But a browse through the daily news on his mobile phone took precedence. This was a morning habit of his rather than genuine curiosity or a need to be up to date with current affairs. The headlines might provide an excuse to explain obstructions to gainful employment in the near future. 'Honey, they're all asking for three years' experience … how the hell can I get experience without getting a … and the internship market, pure slavery, no way. Hang on, now, are you saying you'd do it? No, I didn't think so.' He always had his lines rehearsed.

The option to shower was dismissed for safety reasons. Best rise and leave her domain now. Technically, he lived at another house, sharing it with two people. Aspirations of owning a place of his own were on hold. There was no great hurry. Why bother buying right now when the other pair barely stayed at home? They were still young enough to bleed their parents financially for the next five years, at least. He was the boss of the house by default; they had waived their rights by their absence, which routinely allowed the Sub to stay some nights with his girlfriend and have some nights to himself. It was always important to have a good sanctuary, somewhere to lie low whenever things got tense.

The option to shower right then was dismissed once more. He could have one at his own home after he collected his welfare benefit. If he was still flat out in bed at her place when she returned, she would happily destroy him. Any other day he'd have stayed in bed at least another two hours, but a wallet filled with welfare would briefly make him feel equal to all wage earners. Buying basic goods without having to coin-count before reaching the corner shop was rare. He'd never been caught on a supermarket camera in this town. To stand behind others with so little in his basket belittled him. No, not today, not for this day-to-day grocer. She bought plenty for them both.

It was safe to rise and fulfil his role. He was required to queue with the unfortunate segments of his educated generation, all of whom were primed for positions that existed in cities somewhere else. Motivation levels should be several notches up but for the saturated-market excuses. That reality served him well until he was ready to change. Avoiding recommended training for the last five years had seen the economy come full circle. This did not cause him to jump for joy. 'Just go and get a proper job for feck sake! You're making me look like a waster too,' were the words she had waited to scream at him. Her rage correlated with her career aspirations: both were without limits. The walk to the social welfare office would give him enough time to conjure up a number of plausible defences.

Stumbling downstairs he tugged clothes onto his skinny body, sensitive to front-door creaks. Best be agile and prepared for nasty surprise attacks today. No audible warnings from her hammering heels announced her outside. She could be heard a mile away in slippers whenever she was furious. He wouldn't put it past her to slip back into the house barefoot to catch him, though.

Halfway towards the kitchen with the bright idea to have a cup of tea, he stopped in his tracks. Better not tempt fate. Waiting for a kettle to boil would leave him exposed. Safety first. His jacket was draped across the shoulders of a kitchen chair all ready to be rescued. A set of keys glared at him from the kitchen table; she would be back to collect them at any moment.

He poked his head out the front door. No sign (left or right) of trouble in the immediate vicinity. Body check and pat-down of jacket pockets to see if he had his keys and wallet, a security measure he always went through when departing her house, especially if he had annoyed her. It meant fewer excuses and not having to bribe his way back into her favour with flowers. At forty, having had no job for five unmotivated years, he was by no means a catch. Marriage might interfere with the most up to date version of his master plan. Did he need her as much as she needed him? No. She didn't want to be unmarried at thirty-five.

There would be no grief if he dumped her. No hostility towards him from her or the community that she honestly believed held her in such high regard. Should this bother him? Not really. He never got into that type of popularity game. Sure, he had played it, but he never quite got why it was so important. Getting good grades in college, securing a proper job, marrying, having kids, a house, a car—it all seemed too predictable and linear. Freedom was choice, but for some reason, the majority chose to be held captive by so many external forces. Five years on welfare might have stretched the limits of others goodwill. The tantrum this morning was a wakeup call warning him that his life was due an unwanted surprise.

While walking to receive his welfare benefit, he dwelt on his online game strategy more than his girlfriend strategy. In reality, the latter was more like gaming with some beers instead of a true girlfriend-focused strategy. Game over girlfriend. He would provoke her anger to initiate the break-up later. First he'd text her to get the negative ball rolling. She knew when he was playing on her weakness, but luckily for him, it was usually after the fact. Maybe he'd throw in the old reliable, that the two of them needed some space. He'd tell her before being spotted entering or leaving one of the pubs. That would work for him. She did not do surprises very well. She was not going to like this at all, not unless she organised the split herself. Honesty can be offensive in a society based on image. He had no problem convincing himself that he was the victim here just because he had been brought up to look after number one.

The short journey to the welfare office started from his girlfriend's house; it was nearer, and she usually demanded Monday nights free from him while she recovered from a weekend of image management. Last night he'd stayed over to shelter from constant downpours, which reliably visited the town when promised. The morning showed definite signs of rain too. A view of the mountains would indicate how much rain. Bad weather started usually above them and maneuvered towards the town by lunchtime. Dole, shower, breakfast, and gaming—that was his plan.

Today, he would change his route and saunter past her office. A small display of arrogance or bravery? Darkened clouds suggested that his short jacket might not be able to weather the forecasters' predictions. Last night the rain made it necessary to take a taxi; today he could only afford to walk. Not to worry. The Sub was unusually warm and content inside, empowered by empty streets. Smugness personified, with headphones on, walking towards sinister clouds and imagining his role in euphoric film endings. To any passer-by, he might appear to have just got engaged. A fever had broken; the thought of signing off welfare had crossed his mind again. Today he would simply ask for all employment options and expect suspicious looks from the face behind hatch ten.

The most popular assessment of the Sub was that of an intelligent waster. She, in fairness, could match him. She only went out with him because he had the nerve to ask her and it suited her not to be single. His having the ingenuity to break up with her first was unthinkable. There would be a tantrum followed by foul language (highly charged but accurate) until some form of physical abuse arose, a default setting when words failed her. An attempted kick or punch before she bit her lip. Anger management was absolutely no use on her. He might have to go abroad for his personal safety. Her own family had warned him, half serious, to be prepared. They were cool. He liked to mix with them. But now it was time to show everyone a new, upgraded version of himself. Rise to the challenge today. He decided his time was now.

There was no evidence to others that his thoughts had taken this path. Anyone familiar with his predictable patterns would barely recognise him soon. Would that bother him? If this break-up went badly, it would only fuel his determination to change and solidify an already inflated confidence. As he crossed the street, the Sub became conscious of the energy, the command and rhythm, of his stride. There was more purpose to his walk today, more faith in his footing. He might have been walking towards what he needed all along. Press on; decide later.

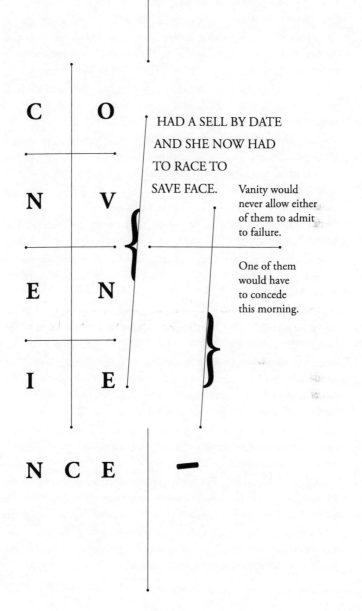

C O N V E N I E N C E

HAD A SELL BY DATE
AND SHE NOW HAD
TO RACE TO
SAVE FACE.

Vanity would
never allow either
of them to admit
to failure.

One of them
would have
to concede
this morning.

The emotional consequences or impact on others of his decision-making process were never going to be dwelt on too deeply. Nothing like this had ever bothered him before. Threats to his preferences were immediately ignored or dismissed with a comical swiftness until every attack on his ego had passed.

The Sub showed no awareness that he was being observed by his next ex from several car lengths behind. About time his world got a shock, she thought. A sense of responsibility far from the comfort of this bubble of his. Rain had been predicted and dark skies agreed. She'd abort her mission and play the long game. Decisiveness in the office was one thing, but dumping him properly was a different type of management. Flat footsteps on flagstones and measured skips onto pavement kerbs confirmed his location. He was the one in ten that was about to leave the dole queue. The Sub had reached that dangerous point where he needed money to get off the dole before it took him another five years to find a sense of motivation to rejoin the work force. He'd do it today. It might make him accept less from himself and others if he were dependent on it for much longer. The sight of the welfare office one street ahead made him anticipate the lifeless face of the lady behind the protective glass of hatch ten. He pictured her holding his immediate future in her hands, which annoyed him. The same meaningless tone of voice, broken by the repetition of the same lifeless information each month, again and again. Next!

A street in the midst of hard times absolved him from his current status. It was 80 per cent derelict, 17 per cent visually assaulted by two generations of teen angst, and 3 per cent mind your own business. Used as a shortcut home with a twist, it was a lesson on the difference between existence and living. Three minutes walking distance from the beginning to the end of this red-bricked neglect. Persecuted windowpanes and kicked-in doors looked away from pedestrian witnesses. A street that never encouraged people to stop and chat for a moment. A street in the process of being erased. Ironically, it was named Mercy Street.

Lumbering charcoal clouds could carry no more moisture, and it would not be long before they informed the town of their true potential. A torrential downpour. Anybody within twenty steps of their destination would curse their reasons for delaying their morning departure. Those running late for important appointments now had lame ice breakers and rain-based excuses to explain away their wrinkled attire. After a few minutes, intermittent shafts of intense sunlight broke their way through windblown curtains of cloud. Light and darkness, jostling for position in a shrinking sky that would return to full visibility a little later on.

She was always in full self-preservation mode when she watched him from a safe distance. Cloud formations informed her of how much time she had left before her attire was reduced to that wet paper bag look. She did not want to get caught like an unsuspecting tourist by the tide at the beach. This tracker would get no answers yet. A break-up seed had been planted in her mind, and the right opportunity had presented itself. She would not be seen as a failure, but as the person who had unfortunately invested more time in a doomed relationship than her partner. 'Beyond the call of duty,' colleagues would say when pushed to ask what was wrong.

Just before she called a halt to her manhunt and turned to leave, she observed her target stop to check his pockets. Finally, her chance to see him face the music. She willed him to stop stalling and search for his wallet. He patted himself down with a systematic flurry as if a small fire in his jacket had to be extinguished. On confirming that his wallet was with him his shoulders relaxed and returned to his walking pace. He had never been the brightest penny in the morning. All she wanted was to witness his facial expression when he opened the note in his wallet. This was enough for her to escape from this dead-end relationship. He wouldn't know what had hit him. The excuses would be epic. Her name would not be dragged through mud of this man's making. Not with a promotion at work imminent. The Sub had become a dangerous liability to her future plans.

The only people in town that the Sub saluted on sight were ones he'd never engaged with socially or ripped off. He kept up appearances with these people for future scams. They contributed to his facade when he was walking around town. His butcher and the elderly assistant at the shop where he bought his cigarettes were the only pair to return his wave. They seemed distracted or slightly reluctant to wave today. The Sub reasoned that Monday was a notoriously difficult day of the week for the average person. It wasn't the first time he had sensed that others were envious of his carefree approach to life. They had chosen their own paths, and there was no reason for him to take their distance personally. After his last benefit cheque, none of this would matter.

The social welfare building had no cascade of steps to trot up, like some city hall lawyer late for court in a detective movie. The dark clouds pushed hard to catch up with his quickened pace. He made it to the front door just as the heavens opened. Inside, the attendees searched for their hatch on their first visit and never again until they either found work or died. For over five years, the Sub had treated the welfare office as a minor inconvenience. It never intimidated him to take state benefit when he was clearly capable of working in the real world. The queue for hatch ten had stalled. It appeared that the person at the head of the line was pleading for humanity with a computer printout in hand.

This was a recurring nightmare for the Sub, to be trapped in a stationary line of strangers that he couldn't prime or make pliable as a group. It had never worked when he tried to get into nightclubs as a kid. For the next five minutes, those preceding him stared at mobile phones, hoping someone would text and not remind them of their responsibility to a society based on finding money to pay the bills. The loud voice at the head of the queue grew weary and finally wore out, allowing for a slow collective shuffle towards hatch ten. The Sub checked his watch whenever he felt trapped. Telling that cold female face behind hatch ten that he had plans was a risk he had to take.

The most coveted word, 'Next!' was being repeated at an upbeat pace. It continued until hatch ten had become visible above the shaved heads of three young men in front of him. The tall trio appeared to be close friends or had accidentally met at the same sports shop. They arrived together and had probably been dismissed from the same place of employment together. The Sub began to prepare for his social security card to be requested. He never remembered which pocket his wallet was hiding in because there was rarely anything of importance in it. Quick hands moved to locate it with an automatic gasp to convince others that he may have lost it. With feigned relief, he located it in the front left-hand side pocket of his jacket. Opening it, he saw its contents had acquired a new member.

His gut instinct told him that his girlfriend's behaviour earlier this morning probably had something to do with this new addition. That muted tantrum in her kitchen and the surprise in his wallet could only mean he'd have to punch above his weight later on. Risks never bothered him much, and consequences even less. 'Next!' Hatch ten illuminated a red sign to inform all, whether they wanted to be there or not, there was only one protocol. The Sub wrestled with the idea of opening and reading the foreign note but removed his social security card for presentation instead. The remaining young man of the trio turned to see his friends politely waiting for him at the front door. 'Next!' Hatch ten called him with familiar disdain. The Sub projected a picture of professionalism, his social security card presented for inspection. The middle-aged face behind the security glass expelled a sigh at the sight of the worst candidate for social reform she had dealt with in ten years. The Sub figured that the job had become meaningless to her shortly before he started signing on at hatch ten. She shoved the slip towards him without a word. He knew the drill but made sure to exaggerate his thanks for her effort. He rattled off his superstar signature onto the slip of paper while smirking at her. She reached to retrieve the slip, but he quickly prevented her by slapping his hand down on it. Her startled eyes bugged, and her jaw nearly dropped.

Hatch ten at the social welfare office had never been eventful, not in his five years of visits, and she was not expecting anything different today. She was the same welfare officer behind the same pair of glasses. They were not bought for style, and they helped her sustain a consistent and reliable stare. A quick watch-check and forced cough announced that his time at the head of the queue had come to an end. He tried to cut an imposing frame in the reflective glass partition and was prepared to pose in front of her for as long as his business took. This got her attention, but she did not reveal it outwardly. She fixed him a look and got the impression he wanted something new. Five years of his attitude would make it hard to change her assessment of him now. The Sub requested signing-off procedures and advice on the possibility of internships. This sat her back in her chair. She was curious but quickly realised that everything hatch ten stood for needed to see the back of him badly. A leaflet with the website details and contacts was pleasantly pushed towards him. Speaking softly, with such unusual warmth that he could only imagine how long she had despised him, she explained the leaflet thoroughly. 'God willing, I'll be back to sign off in a week, and I'll be out of your hair for good' were his parting words.

With so many familiar faces, the Sub was always conscious of how he appeared when departing the welfare building. In his mind, he was just dropping something off. The downpour had passed over, leaving the blocked drains unable to absorb excess water. Waving farewell to the welfare building, he turned and wondered where he could read the mysterious note in private. Get cigarettes first, a ritual he enjoyed after receiving his benefit. Paying for twenty cigarettes, he separated the note from his wallet and slid it into his back pocket. Stepping outside the shop, he lit up and inhaled his first of the day. The folded curiosity could be opened now. His photograph appeared beside a photocopy of a fake €20 note with the details from local bars to watch out for both. On the flip side, a filthy handwritten warning was scrawled by her brother. The Sub weighed up his options. It was high time for him to move on.

CHAPTER

9

INCOMING

| | | | | | | | | |0|

" "

Restoration of the self was the most important purpose of a night's sleep, a fundamental human necessity, according to his father. Waking from an unsatisfactory sleep left Ninja disorientated, groggy, and unsure about which day of the week it was. Dream fragments shied away from the earliest probes of daylight, suggesting consciousness would ask for a shot at the day soon. Curtain-edge gaps failed to defend his bedroom walls from the gradual investigation by the sun. Summer had officially resumed its claim on his early mornings. Another ten-minute snooze was futile. Dream time had been upset and forgotten fast. One memory remained and could not be forgotten. The artist formally known as Ninja Paddy had finally died on stage last night.

Reach for the curtain, a stretch and peek to check that his van was still facing the back door of the house. It had sat parked in the same place since the previous day's excursion. The mechanical heap of reliable loyalty had become the only confidant Ninja spoke to throughout his charitable work. It never questioned his decisions to take to the road. The van accepted its role willingly, regardless of rain, shine, sleet, or occasional snow. It never failed to start on the first turn. Always good to go. They had learned to do their best work together.

He had found it difficult to leave his bed yesterday morning. From the neck down, his body felt like it had been vacuum-packed by his quilt, leaving his face exposed to stare motionless at the ceiling. Their final Sunday run had ended sadly. His father lay sleeping in the next room in a similar position.

He lay in some other universe, one that may not make sense to others. Ninja had begun to think of the injustice of having to take responsibility for a life that had only been partially revealed to either of his sons. Their father couldn't remember all of his own achievements, could he? Not now that Alzheimer's came calling. Could his brother and he continue their father's legacy at the expense of their own attempts to succeed? It was time to inform his brother of his decision to retire from charity work, the only aspect of his identity that locals were never likely to take responsibility for.

Filling the cultural void created by last night's on-stage resignation was not going to prove too difficult. Ninja figured they'd just flick on the TV. The Ninja Paddy brand was not on par with Ziggy Stardust. Ninja had always envisioned his own career, unlike Mr. Bowie's, as a brief one, a career destined to disappear if his personal life required it. The idea of the revered Mr. Bowie hauling DJ equipment in Ziggy attire raised a borderline smile. For some time, Ninja had feared bar costume had become too familiar—frayed and unable to turn heads anymore. To make matters worse, Ninja's final gig coincided with the local football teams' promotion to league one. The jubilant parade of returning car horns sounded his own demotion. What a send-off.

He had spent the last night playing the fool in front of people that had laughed hard at similar comic material before but claimed to know better now—a final performance that would have generated appalling reviews based on the audience's reaction. They had found a new interest that day in their local GAA team, which had pulled off an impressive and unexpected win. Long-term football rival, Bally Mac Robin, were beaten up and down the pitch. Ninja could not compete with this minor football frenzy. Side profiles that were oblivious to his performance was a signal that he had finished before he'd even got started. The locals didn't value entertainment that sold itself for free, and charity had become intrusive. Nobody noticed his stage departure. Ninja stood at the end of the bar counter with a neck towel, waiting to knock a glass of still water back in one.

Dennis knew Ninja was waiting. He let him wait. The adrenalin wore off Ninja rapidly as he realised that everyone at the bar appeared to have been served. Ninja told him he'd collect his gear the next day. 'OK?' he asked, unsure if he was working the Monday afternoon shift. Dennis told him to take the day off by flapping his hands in a dismissive way. He was not needed there anymore. That was the moment that bugged Ninja the most. He had lost all respect for his boss right then. That depressing thought forced him to sit up and bury his head in the palms of his hands.

Strange sounds of movement distracted Ninja from wallowing. They emanated from close by. He heard his father's voice speak through his bedroom wall in confused tones and childlike panic. The anxiety in the old man's monologue encouraged Ninja to rise from his bedside, drag his jeans on, and assess the situation. No need to barge in. He placed his ear against the door and tried not to frighten the man out of his remaining wits. The moment to enter his father's room had passed. Ninja waited outside in silence. The house suspended its structural creaks to back up Ninja's shallow breathing. A single-knuckle knock gently announced his presence. 'Is everything alright there … Dad?' Ninja asked softly.

Slippers shuffled across the wooden floor and slowed up softly nearer the door. Ninja waited nervously for his father to complete the journey and twist the door handle. The door opened with just enough space for a single eye to peep through. The old man stared at Ninja's concerned face before shutting the door. 'Who are you?' whispered his father, and again once more.

To help calm his father down, Ninja thought quickly and tried to give some family references to get the old man's bearings back in check. Having a nickname for so many years did not help Ninja's cause. Confused but less frightened, his father recognised his eldest son's name when Ninja mentioned it. After more reassurance, he allowed his forgotten son to escort him downstairs to get some breakfast. This was the beginning of the end and Ninja knew it.

For the next few hours, his father drifted between the man that he and his brother knew and one whose faltering memory left Ninja without an identity. Ninja watched his father relax at the kitchen table while he washed the breakfast plates. He needed to rethink all previous plans. Showing Bart photographs might upset the memories that Ninja wanted to leave intact. He'd tell his brother to forget the issue of the photographs upstairs. Who are you? Ninja wondered why his father had forgotten his name. This hurt. Even allowing for the old man's unfortunate decline, this hurt Ninja bad. He would rather not talk about the episode with his brother.

A mid-morning breath of air tossed the kitchen curtain; it was likely the front door had opened. A female voice that hadn't been heard in several months said, 'Anyone home? It's only me.' Her seductive voice swept away any emotional dust that lay in their mother's kitchen. The old man twitched, recognising the tone, and called out her name immediately. His elder son had married a catch, a goading remark directed at Ninja, usually each time the darling couple departed for Dublin. The younger son never fell for his father's bait to settle down. His father knew it, too, which was exactly why he said it. Ninja concentrated on his sister-in-law's first reaction to the old man sitting in his dressing gown, his chin bristling with white stubble. He watched her drop her bag and quick step across the kitchen floor to kiss her father-in-law without hesitation. His brother leant in sideways to gauge if his intervention were needed. 'Honey, I just need to speak to Ninja for a minute. You'll be alright here with Dad?' he said, winking weirdly at Ninja.

She instinctively began to fuss over her father-in-law and comfortably waved the two brothers away. She knew the score. There had always been genuine affection between her and the old man. The downstairs hallway was the best place for privacy when the kitchen door was fully closed. Ninja nodded his head and explained in detail what had happened earlier. He admitted he wouldn't be able to take care of him. The old man might not be able to remember either of their names soon. Only big city finances could help out when the doctor's final opinion came. The last few hours had drained conversation out of Ninja, and he excused himself to go into town for groceries.

'Sure thing, Ninja. Maybe get some extra food so we can all have dinner together here. We'll be staying the rest of the week at the hotel.' His brother never said much, unless you read into it. Ninja nodded in the direction of his animated wife. The female laughter emanating from the kitchen was warm and infectious. His brother forced a ball of banknotes into Ninja's palm. It met with no resistance. He turned to grab his keys and made his way to the van.

Twirling keys around his index finger was a positive sign. This was no charity run, for a change, and he gave the van an 'easy boy' pat on the front grill. His van didn't need to know about its master's morning, not this morning. It had never paid heed before. Key in the ignition, ready to fire up the motor. Click. Silence. Ninja rolled his eyes upwards, lay his forehead gently on the steering wheel, and prayed for patience. A delayed breath and another tentative turn of the key, and the motor kicked into action. 'Thank you, buddy, thank you. But could'ya please play ball? I'm begging you, just help me out. I don't need any more grief today.' The face-off with his reflection in the windscreen mirror ended in a tie. No upbeat facade to be seen anywhere in it.

His sister-in-law took her leave from the kitchen table laughter and frantically waved out at Ninja from the window. Ninja was about to wave back until he realised that she was beckoning him to wait until she made it out the back. He assumed she needed something from the supermarket and watched her politely skip her way to the passenger door. 'Ninja, it's just that I wanted to say something. It's no big deal,' she said with her head down before composing herself. 'I guess himself told you we're having a bit of trouble. It's nothing, Ninja. Just wanted to say that we're going to … Everything should work out just fine, it's just a glitch. You OK with that?'

He was happy that she felt comfortable telling him. His smile said so and she was happy to see it. Watching the van leave, she figured Ninja was being honest with her. He hadn't a mean bone in his body. A rapid burst of the horn let her return safely to the kitchen knowing he was cool with her too.

Getting involved with his brother's personal business was not a good idea. It was up to each of them to sort their own problems out first. It was a family rule. His trusty van avoided adding grief to Ninja's morning by remaining quiet. What had just happened amazed Ninja to the point of distraction. Years had gone by without this amount of emotional traffic, and never in one morning. He'd never run from that house, its occupants, or its troubles.

HIS FATHER ONCE SAID

"

JUDGE A PERSON

BY THEIR ACTIONS.

"

Somehow today

was an assessment

point and not

Consider modifications and

a definite end.

detours en route but only

if change decides to make

life uncomfortable.

As much as Ninja liked to be in the middle of activity, he did not go out of his way to seek stressful situations. Nobody was at fault here; he just wasn't experienced enough in dealing with stress. Because of this he got distracted easily and forgot that life made up new rules for its playbook constantly. Ninja badly needed the revised edition. He could count himself lucky that up until now he'd had a good family and a bar job at least. The Sunday run, that one activity in his public life that made him valuable to others, was a closed chapter now. The exploits of Ninja Paddy were canned, as of last night.

A dashboard red light made its presence known. Ninja could not remember the last time that a warning light had ever occurred. 'Now you're just messing with me. Seriously … are you trying to say there's actually something wrong? Is this meant to be some cry for help? Give me a break.' The mirror reflected a pair of eyes in disbelief. Having to worry about his beloved van was new territory. Had he been taking it for granted? Was it trying to teach him a lesson? The warning light continued. Split glances from the light to the road had him calculating the distance to town and the chances of a breakdown. If the problem was serious, he'd have to get it fixed on arrival. The warning light and the distance from town forced his hand. He chose not to floor it. 'Hang in there, buddy! I'll have to have words with you whenever we make it home. Get your act together,' he demanded.

All that was missing from the drama was radio chatter from a control tower to talk his craft gently into town. The van was nursed carefully to town and slipped into a parking space directly across the street from the supermarket. The vehicle stayed silent as Ninja locked the driver's door behind him. Nobody else shopped with such matter-of-fact impatience. The staff knew exactly how much of the shopping trolley he would fill. Shopping was not his bag. The girls at the cash registers liked to bet on how fast he'd fill the trolley. Ninja remarked he'd like be out of their lives quicker. He was halfway down aisle three before a displeased, 'Be nice, Ninja, or else …' could be heard over the intercom speakers.

Before Ninja could navigate his trolley around the corner at the far end of aisle three, he was met by the sound of a familiar chuckle. 'Well, Dennis, is it yourself?' asked Ninja, pulling his cart to a halt. Dennis was holding a dozen lemons in a plastic bag, a chore he usually left to Ninja. He giggled, waving a weighing scale sticker stuck to his index finger. Ninja wondered whether he should ask about his employer's attitude as he was leaving the gig last night.

'Are you giving those lovely ladies a hard time, Ninja?'

Ninja explained that they teased each other on an ongoing basis. 'It gets them through the daily tedium.' As a deflection, Ninja leant low on his trolley and asked Dennis if he'd be interested in taking the sound system off his hands, for the bar. Dennis considered himself a master dealmaker. He was put on the spot in aisle three and began to construct a diplomatic dialogue in his head. It forced his facial muscles to furrow his brow. It unnerved Ninja enough to expect that there was bad news heading his way. Dennis had given that look before he gives bar staff a reduced shift rota.

'Well, my good friend, now that you happen to mention it, I've been thinking, Ninja,' he said. These words were delivered with unusual delicacy for a man who had trouble holding his tongue. A new direction was being taken, one that had no room in it for Ninja as a barman now that Ninja Paddy was no longer performing. Ninja sensed the news was not the good type. 'I'm going to have to let you go from the bar, Ninja. I just don't have the work. Summer … unfortunately has been worse than dead.'

All of Ninja's instincts were hitting home now. He asked his former boss if he would be back in the bar in an hour so he could drop in and collect his gear. Dennis cautiously nodded, unsure if Ninja was in denial or if his words had not sunk in yet.

The girl sitting at the checkout observed Ninja's fast pace along the last aisle. He may have offended her earlier but she waved him over. He looked back in the direction of Dennis and shook his head. 'Can't please everyone these days,' she said. He wondered if she knew what had happened on aisle three, beside the lemons.

He never lost his temper, never became unruly or violent in front of others. Never had that killer instinct or knockout gene, but after this morning he was beginning to ask himself what harm it would do if he lashed out once in a while? His trolley refused to remain stationary by the side door of the van. It wrestled with him as he inserted the van key. Eventually he tamed it before placing the groceries inside. The last thing he wanted was commentary from his guests about the condition of the groceries or his hazardous method of shopping. He must have had a face like a beetroot leaving the cash register. God knows what the checkout girl's final assessment of him would be at their closing time chinwag.

The side door of the van refused to shut cleanly until some calm, polite force eventually stepped in to take control of Ninja's temperament. As Dennis left the supermarket, he told Ninja to meet him at the bar whenever he was ready. A deep inhalation calmed him as he nodded politely in reply.

How can that man be so calm? Ninja wondered. Their time together in the bar was just a show? Was there any mutual respect?

Sitting in the van, it seemed to Ninja that today was a test, and he would soon wake up from it in a cold sweat. His luck was never this bad; it could not last. Keys in the ignition. One turn, no start. Then a three-word engine prayer. It started.

The red dashboard light started to blink straight away. He'd deal with it after he'd collected the gear from Dennis. This was not the time to be annoyed. He wanted to curse with intense sincerity. The van made its way up the town after Dennis. It didn't take Ninja long to remove any trace of last night's efforts to entertain the locals. He had enough motivation this morning. Alone inside the bar, he felt like apologising to the empty premises for trying to help out, but it seemed his efforts were never going to amount to much. He called out for Dennis before he shut the front door. After a moment of silence, he just closed the door behind him and made for the privacy of the van. His life had been a charmed one up until now, but what would come next?

Ninja heard his name being called from out of sight. For a split second of positivity he thought that Dennis might have had a change of heart. Nope, it was his graphic designer friend giving him a wave from his studio doorway. The van could wait. The man known to have bundles of energy walked across the street with lumbering steps. It was difficult for his friend to distinguish whether Ninja was fatigued from another late night or furious for some other reason. His friend knew better than to waste Ninja's time with idle talk. He asked Ninja if he would be around later and mentioned that he had a bit of bad news to tell him.

Ninja lit into him. 'You? You think you've had a bit of bad news? Let me tell you, buddy, that whatever bad news you think you've got, I'll fecking bury it with woe so high that they'll have to reclassify Everest.' As soon as the flow of words could be forced to stop he fell into embarrassed silence. His friend apologised for assuming Ninja would always be his trademark good-humoured self.

'I'm sorry, I apologize I've just a few things on my mind that have messed up my world. Dude, I'll get back to you whenever I can get myself sorted, and, believe me, it's ... oh, never mind,' Ninja said, still ashamed of his earlier loss of composure.

The designer realised at that moment that he was truly out of touch with Ninja's life. He'd never seen him this stressed before. Ninja had never intentionally been mean, and his friend took no offence. He heard that Ninja had finished up with the Ninja Paddy experience last night and figured that they should have a chat about what would happen next. Ninja agreed before making his way back to the van. It started, the red light blinked, and he drove off troubled. He never expected so much crap to hit in such a condensed time frame. Thoughts of the dole, at fifty years of age, would have to be revised in some way to make it a practical choice, a positive option. He drove in the direction of the social welfare office. Feck Dennis. A trickle of people walked down the street towards him. Standing outside a corner shop, he saw the Sub studying a piece of paper intensely.

He would go to the welfare office tomorrow. Best get home with the groceries and see what was happening back at the ranch. This logic could not hide the fact that queuing behind the Sub would be annoying to him. Ninja wondered if today's unexpected events would be easier to deal with if he were the Sub. Things had not got as bad as that, had they? What if he had been given a brass neck transplant from the Sub? Could he sail through life without the consequences of having a conscience? Ninja knew he would have to expect, and deal with, locals' disgust at his leaving the Sunday run. How would he deal with their disappointment and avoid a public lynching? It wasn't even eleven o'clock in the morning.

Who are you? The fear of being invisible or forgotten by his father put priorities back in order again. Suck it up, Ninja. You have got to suck it up or it will take you down with it. Passing by Dennis, he rolled down his window to shout that he had got his gear, but no words would come out. His former employer's face was slightly red as he considered whether Ninja had listened to him earlier in the supermarket. No point in trying to read the thoughts of his blushing ex-boss; he was content with the knowledge that he had nothing to be ashamed of. A small sign of appreciation for working in Maguire's would have been nice but nothing was offered. There would be no more pints with his brother in Maguire's.

He pulled in behind the house, and once again his sister-in-law left the kitchen table to politely skip out and meet him. 'That was really quick, Ninja; wish you'd do my shopping!' She laughed without any hint of insincerity. He was about to turn the engine off, but the red light continued to blink. He was annoyed enough to try and figure the mystery out; it couldn't be avoided any longer. He reached across to the glove compartment to search for answers in the van manual, fumbled through rubbish, and found it. On retrieval, he noticed a small handwritten message attached.

'Dear Ninja, if I were twenty years younger ... Thank you for showing us a little of your world. Love, Irene and Glenn.' Ninja noticed that the red warning light had stopped blinking.

CHAPTER

10

PLANS

( )

'Don't worry, the Ninja show is all over, my friend. No more Meals on Wheels or bar performances. All that money you're owed will be in your greedy little pocket by next Monday afternoon. How's that for slick business, my graphic design buddy?' said an upbeat Ninja.

He entered his friend's studio without bothering to check if there were any clients present. It was not a very big town. There was only one trained and qualified designer in the vicinity that wasn't a pixel pusher, and luckily he was a good friend to Ninja.

'Catch!' Ninja roared, while throwing a packet of biscuits at his friend, along with the mid-air warning that they might be out of date soon. His friend's arms struggled awkwardly to cradle the pack.

Luke erupted from his focused stare with a barrage of outrageous profanities. Ninja raised both hands to surrender Smiling nervously, he stepped back and apologised needlessly for all sorts, but it didn't help to soften the mood. It was more frustration than coherent abuse. His friend finally deflated back onto his swivel chair, kicked his shoes off, and lowered his head. He had been beaten down by business before. Ninja reminded him that it was he who had asked him to come by. There were difficult times ahead of both of them, and they needed to plan. The kettle was filled for distraction, and Ninja waited respectfully for some cue to speak. To break the tension, he remarked on how many people liked the last poster, The Nine Lives of Ninja.

Another soothing comment was badly needed. It might probe this man's anger and reveal its severity. His friend leaned forward from his chair and reached into the waste paper basket for a balled-up piece of paper which clearly still played on his mind. Some news unfortunately could not be disposed of so easily. He began to unfold it, unhappy to reread its contents again. His expression implied that it would be unpleasant, but this was not the time to freak out. The air thinned, waiting for a truckload of sorrow to announce itself from the little pebble of paper. 'West Com to cease trading,' read the printout. The golden goose was dead; it would not be long before his design pool would surely run dry.

Ninja decided to take responsibility for making tea for both of them. He seemed to think better while doing something, and luckily for him, there never seemed to be a clean cup around when he paid a visit. Somewhere, hiding in a shanty town of plates, saucers, and cereal bowls, must be some stained teacups to wash. This was just the physical manifestation of a creative mind, according to Luke. Once a design job came in, he immersed himself in it. The effort employed was based on the nature of the problem, time scale, client preference, and trust. He'd always applied himself wholeheartedly to each design at the expense of all other personal distractions.

Luke was committed to the process of solving design problems regardless of changes made by his client base. Ninja knew when to nod quietly in agreement. Requests that disregarded any theory of visual communication he believed to be true were avoided. The two had become close friends over several years. Staying silent for a few moments was not an issue for concern.

The office phone rang unexpectedly but was left to ring out. Tea cups were stamped onto the sink decking until no more could safely add to the regimented pattern. Ninja, tea towel in hand, turned to the dejected face and decided to wipe the issue clean in one fell swoop. 'What would you like to design right now?' he asked. 'Is there a project that would satisfy you? One that would reward you for all your training? Realistically?' At first these questions did not appear to have registered, but they did sink in eventually and snap his friend out of his gloom. He hauled his frame out of his seat with slow majesty to show his friend a personal project. This idea had liberated his questioning spirit, a spirit that had once been clamped down by the secondary school formula of spoon-feeding. Cautiously walking to his desk, he turned to check for signs of ridicule from Ninja. A long roll of paper was drawn out in a fashion that implied that it was a rare privilege to witness. Instinctively Ninja cleared a table space large enough to accommodate the project. He stared at the project fully unfurled, his eyes large with potential, and let the man of passion speak without interruption.

silence

Can you hear it?

L ¡ S † ³ ń

Can't you hear anything at all?

It's all around you, can't find anything around you without it and yet you can't hear it?

m e s s a g e
m e a n i n g
c o m m u n i c a t i o n

|GRAPHIC DESIGN|

c r e a t i v i t y |IS|
e v o l u t i o n
p s y c h o l o g y
s o u l
|MUSIC| l a n g u a g e
e m o t i o n

C O N T R O L
| counter | PHILOSOPHY | revolution |
M Y T H O L O G Y
| ELITISM | IGNORANCE | EXCLUSION | PREJUDICE | FEAR | GREED |
R E L A T I V I T Y

& for the visually adventuous
chronically curious.

| e | m | e | r | g | e | n | c | e |

NOT JUST SIGNS AND STUFF?

THE POWER   *It can convey meaning in a way that*

WHICH MUSIC   *speaks to us when we do not possess the*

INSTILS, ITS   *words to express what we mean to say*

EMOTIVE   *to others or how we want them to feel.*

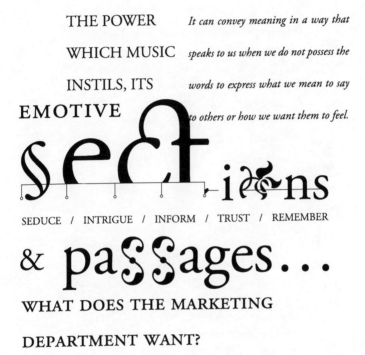

sections

SEDUCE / INTRIGUE / INFORM / TRUST / REMEMBER

& passages...

WHAT DOES THE MARKETING

DEPARTMENT WANT?

CHOPSTICKS!

| d | i | v | e | r | g | e | n | c | e |

MORE THAN SIGNS AND STUFF?

The spoken word is our favorite mode of communication. We never get bored of listening to how great we were at our verbal gymnastics. There's far too much talk now and no plans for action. Soon we'll have nothing to say and we'll mimic the design of all those who never understood us.

s   i   l   e   n   c   e

No creative questioning anymore, style over form over function these days? Our visual language will always need to be conscious of current trends in consumer speak. Advertising and branding taglines will jostle to be heard across many more platforms. We will have to chase the visual language of other countries who have mastered it by evolution. An opportunity knocked on our door in the 70's but we were an island back then. We can't think that way now.

| c | o | n | v | e | r | g | e | n | c | e |

'Trying to explain to the general public that the objective of a poster is to speak, use the space, and not just make things bigger is completely futile,' Ninja was told. 'Being able to see the words or imagery doesn't automatically mean that anyone really wants to read them. People are sensitive to the semiotics of visual communications which are in tune with their emotional state or personal temperament. It's that simple. We tend to gravitate towards graphic design that mirrors our preferences. Research your audience preferences, their fears, their aspirations, and then, with design, you can persuade them to consider your message. Music is allowed to breathe naturally, and good design needs that allowance too. We've grown up in a country which was trained to be aurally sensitive but conditioned to mistrust the visual arts except when they're given merit from abroad. Design theory aside, some clients expect you to copy and paste your way to a solution or mimic their rival company's stock photo library. It could be a long time before a client asks you what you think the best solution is and places their faith in you to design it. Every so often, once in a while,' he emphasized his words by pointing at Ninja, 'a designer gets to create a great solution for an amazing communication problem, but that type of opportunity is scarce these days. I've said my piece.' He returned to slumping in his chair.

Designing free posters for a fundraising maniac who stylized each performance by being embarrassingly good at comedy had been his best work. Work that asked more from him and his creative mindset. Ninja was his client from heaven, allowing his friend to visually communicate without too many restrictions. Many years ago, when the graphic design profession broke away from the art departments of advertising agencies, there had been much more creative freedom. Now it has come full circle with branding agencies. Since then, the accounts managers had diluted the creative process between designer and client by searching for the latest trend rather than the best solution. It seemed that designers couldn't be trusted with too much contact with a client these days.

Ninja had visions of a lounge pianist making a meagre existence from playing piano in some dingy bar. Each night the local punters considered this guy as part of the bar wallpaper. Suddenly this overlooked player pulls up a seat to a Steinway and plays his own classical composition, bewitching the audience. Ninja felt uncomfortable for making so many assumptions about his friend. He was embarrassed enough to hang his head. He hadn't realised how entrenched Luke had become in his work. His profession might be costing him his health. Many of his design peers wouldn't risk half his commitment, but they always seemed to come out on top.

Ninja now understood that money had nothing to do with his friend's disappointment with West Com closing down. What this man needed was a totally unique challenge, a purpose to engage the explorative and creative side of him which the general business community would never request. The two friends hovered over the A0 project, its potential, its personal content, mapped into regions of aesthetic emphasis and timeline context. His friend was exploring a world of typographic understanding but, for some reason, had felt it necessary to keep it neatly tucked away in a drawer, protected from others whom he did not trust to understand. He believed he had conveyed the true essence of his design viewpoint to an appreciative Ninja. 'Never underestimate the power of the viewer to comprehend the design communication process.' He said this with reservation while making sure his friend was listening. Ninja tried to correlate his friend's words with memories of Ninja Paddy posters he had designed in the past. The designer went on to explain that there was much more to it than the dismissive 'signs'n'stuff' mentality. Explanations of the Western reading pattern, semiotics, the hierarchy of information, meaning, tone of voice, style, function, form, colour, aesthetic composition, grid systems, and alignments all gushed out in a spontaneously emotive stream. Ninja's mind baked inside. Luke wiped his glasses and asked him to pass the biscuits. It had become obvious to both of them that they needed a new purpose.

Sometimes it took trauma to glimpse the positive glow of what was truly possible—a collaboration with none of the boundaries of West Com and its house style trappings. The two talked of the message, its context, its meaning, and how the reader should feel by the whole design experience. Ninja would supply all the information. This project would help him say goodbye, a parting gesture to the people he could no longer afford to help. His exit would be visually documented properly. All the previous posters, along with the candid photographs from venues and performances, would be housed in a book. The souls that he had to leave behind might live on in the pages of this project. The years of charity work might be remembered fondly by others this way, but that was not important now. This project and their combined efforts could probably reach more people than ever volunteered to help Ninja in reality. He, the client from heaven, was encouraged to demand more from the design after the message and audience preferences were better defined. Production costs needed to be realistic, but the quality of the product must be premium. West Com's departure may have been a blessing to his friend's health. The final fade-out of Ninja's charitable efforts would at least open an avenue to its aesthetic remembrance.

The popular influence of outsiders and economic powers do the most to change our ways. They make us self-conscious and force us to act to protect our truth as we know it. They can be disliked because of this. Ninja had no other option but to publicly humiliate himself in order to raise awareness of his cause to help the rural elderly. Once he became the last contact (except for the Postman) to liaise between the town and those stationed at isolated outposts, he expected to receive less support from locals. His departure from the Sunday run might devastate the few who had relied on his humanity even more than his choice of biscuits or photographs to rekindle memories that were untouched by progress. By the time the two departed the studio, it was apparent to both of them that their previously folded ideas for change would need to be unpacked carefully from aspirational drawers.

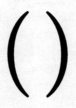

The End

ABOUT THIS BOOK:

Thoughts from disconnected others can randomly affect our future decisions, whether we are aware of them or not. Private interpretations of this life may differ from one set of eyes to the next. Knowing nothing of the personal lives and thoughts of others, we wade through the present together. Individuals have become too busy to realise that they are each just one switch interacting with the countless streams of human connectivity secretly suspending them all. Ten fictional Irish stories observing characters in transition but connected by rural co-dependency, time and place.

THANKS TO:

Seamus Tarpey
Helen Tarpey
Paul Tarpey
Mary McGrath
Hugh Tarpey
Joan Carney

Damien M Harrington
Jenny Trigwell
Giovanna Fregni
Cordula Hansen
Ross Lee
Aisling Boland

Adobe Garamond Pro
Proportional Grid 8/8
4mm Margin & Gutters

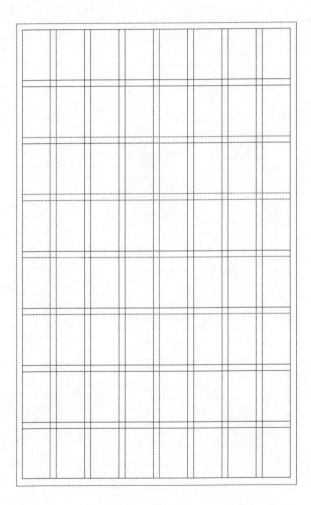

www.johntarpey.com